About the Author

Dennis Reed is a native New Yorker, attended New York City public schools. Mr. Reed taught writing courses at William and Mary, Morehouse College, and worked on his doctorate at Georgia State University. Mr. Reed's book of poetry is entitled *Definitions*. His work has appeared in *College Language Association Journal*, *Essence*, and *Style*, and his memoir, *Migration Memories*, received the North Street Book of the Year. Honorable Mention Award in 2020 and was chosen as a semi-finalist in the NCTE/Norman Mailer Non-Fiction for Teacher's Award in 2014. His screenplay "Love on the Corner," won the fourth place Award from Scriptapalooa in 2020. His analysis of the New York Knicks, *Sell the Team*, was published in 2022 by Olympia Press. This is the first of three of Mr. Reed's novels to be published by Olympia Publishers.

Guerrilla Warfare

Dennis Reed

Guerrilla Warfare

Olympia Publishers
London

www.olympiapublishers.com
OLYMPIA PAPERBACK EDITION

Copyright © Dennis Reed 2024

The right of Dennis Reed to be identified as author of this work has been asserted in accordance with sections 77 and 78 of the Copyright, Designs and Patents Act 1988.

All Rights Reserved

No reproduction, copy or transmission of this publication may be made without written permission.
No paragraph of this publication may be reproduced, copied or transmitted save with the written permission of the publisher, or in accordance with the provisions of the Copyright Act 1956 (as amended).

Any person who commits any unauthorized act in relation to this publication may be liable to criminal prosecution and civil claims for damage.

A CIP catalogue record for this title is available from the British Library.

ISBN: 978-1-80074-589-6

This is a work of fiction.
Names, characters, places and incidents originate from the writer's imagination. Any resemblance to actual persons, living or dead, is purely coincidental.

First Published in 2024

**Olympia Publishers
Tallis House
2 Tallis Street
London
EC4Y 0AB**
Printed in Great Britain

Dedication

I dedicate this book to my wife, Kari, my children, Karma and Keia, and my grandchildren, Richard James III and Zion Reed Morrison.

Acknowledgements

I wish to thank Dr. Dance of the University of Richmond, for her invaluable guidance, my wife for her patience with my theatrical personality, and Dr. Lomax of City University for his guidance and love. The Bud Jones Poets, Mervyn Taylor, Fatisha, Verona, Dr. Delores Williams, and Wesley Brown discovered me. Derek Walcott, the Noble Prize-winning poet, spent time with me; at eighteen, when I was a young man from South Jamaica, with a holey T-shirt and jeans. Special thanks to John Oliver Killens, Toni Morrison, and Toni Cade Bambara and Malaika Adero.

1967
CHAPTER ONE

I found it one day when I was looking for something else. It's a black, dusty ass book, with impressions on the front that look like a tree. But it wasn't until I felt its strong spine that I knew.

This was my journal that I had kept when I was a teenager, back when life seemed clear.
   I crack it open.

> Saw Sandra today from the second-floor window. Her calves quivered as she walked in high heels to her building door. She lives right across from us now, but my fool mother wants to leave the projects and live in a private house. For a long time, I didn't like living in the projects but now I do. Sandra has made all this brick bearable and now I must leave her. The brothers will be on her like white on rice. I really don't want to leave now. I'll wait until when my mother gets tipsy, and then pitch it to her. How everybody was distant when I first moved here and now it feels like home, almost. Mom loses her mind when she drinks. That's why Dad got into book city. So, tonight, when she's good and oiled, I'll make the "don't you want me to be happy?" appeal.

Dinner is noodles and tomato sauce again.

"What are we, Italian?"

"You're lucky you have a nice meal like that. The people overseas wish they could have that kind of meal."

"Well, you could ship it to them."

"Look, boy, if you keep talking like that, I'll leave your Black ass right here when we move."

"That would be fine with me. It took me a long time to make friends here."

"Union Hall is two minutes from 109th Avenue."

"Yeah, but they have a whole new group of kids over there. They don't hang like we do over here."

"That's exactly why I'm moving. You're hanging a little too much. And besides, it's an investment."

"What about all the time I spent breaking down barriers and trying to protect you and me both?"

"I appreciate that, son, but I need something I can hand down to you when I close these eyes."

"Not that again. Think about staying."

"You worry about that skirt across the way? That god damn Sandra."

"It's not just that."

"Then what is it? They got gangs on Union Hall Street but by now you should know who and what to stay away from."

"I'm sure about around here but over at Union Hall Street, I got no clue."

"Just like you broke down the barriers here, you can do it a block or two away. Besides, in a year or two it's graduation and then college and 'later' for these niggers around here."

"You got it all planned out."

"You have to come up with a road map if you're going to get

anywhere."

I could still hear her talking as I ate the last bit, turning into the dark hallway, walking up to my room. Union Hall Street was just a minute away, but it was a world of dark, oversized houses. At least there is excitement within the brick walls of the projects—there are no laws, and drugs are used out in the open. I see black, rectangular boom boxes on bulging shoulders and every night is party night in the square between the two buildings that separate my building from Sandra's. When it is dark, I can see though her bedroom window, and she will pull down the yellow venetian blinds and dance behind it, just for me; I can see her curving shape through the rips in the blinds. Tonight, she backs up, and does a dance move in the shadows, curving and twerking. Her light-brown skin contrasts with the torn shade. Sandra hesitates, to make sure I'm looking. I peer through the dirty smudges of the venetian blinds to see her middle moving and suddenly I am out of the projects, sitting in the front row of a Broadway show, watching Lola Falana. I move to the other side of the bed, up against the glass and just gaze and dream that she is in my room, sliding underneath me, with her muscular bowlegs.

I call her almost every night and set up a time for her to come to the window, doing a professional shimmy that she learned at Performing Arts High School. She is supposed to be one of the best dancers in the city; her sleekness and curving thin sides are what I hold on to when we walk but all of that would be taken away—the soulful shadows of movement, the squares where we hang on benches talking all night, the teenage girls snatching their bodies back from the ravages of pregnancy, and the feeling that no one cares about us. All of that would be gone if I left.

The police are afraid of South Jamaica. They know they can lose their lives and never go home to their families again, like Edward Byrne, the rookie police officer they say was shot by my friend Scott Todd. I saw Scott Todd grow up and he didn't seem like a murderer to me. But he went to work for a drug dealer and the police had the nerve to stake out the drug dealer's house, so Scott Todd was sent on a mission, and he completed his mission, and now he's been in jail for fifty-three years.

Four former crackheads convicted in the 1967 assassination of rookie Queens cop, Edward Byrne, were turned down last week in their bid for freedom.
    Todd Scott and David McClary, who were convicted with two co-conspirators of assassinating Byrne more than 20 years ago, were denied parole following a November 14 interview with the state parole board.
    The panel turned down a bid for freedom by Scott and McClary after NYPD Commissioner Raymond Kelly, Mayor Michael Bloomberg and other officials voiced opposition to their release. Both men are eligible to apply again in November 2014, authorities said. From the NEW YORK DAILY NEWS

After Scott Todd killed officer Byrne, we started to see police around the three and six story buildings known as the South Jamaica housing projects. I had never seen any police officer in South Jamaica, in my life, before.

It is a place of loose behavior; where once the sun goes down anything can occur. Boom boxes come out and the park benches are full, and the universe turns upside down. It is the cloak of night that allows people to become obtuse; no police officer is coming. People come from other neighborhoods to buy drugs and live without the law here.

Crime flourishes because all the elements are here. A lack of employment and a proliferation of drugs. A fourteen-year-old can find the drug dealer's house, but the police can't.

The police don't serve and protect here; they occasionally occupy when there is a major crack bust coming down. The police only put people in jail if it is easy for them to get in and get out of South Jamaica with their suburban lives intact in Bensonhurst or some other part of the city where cops life. They raid the crack dens in the morning when the benches are free. They don't want an audience seeing how they operate. All Black men are guilty. That is a part of the niggerhood I will not miss, but there are good people on the benches, trying to understand this fractious country. They try to understand what lying President Lyndon Baines Johnson is saying without the benefit of high school diplomas or basic civics classes. Johnson, when he comes on television at night, looks worse and worse, as if the war is dragging him down, changing his face and marring his Presidency with the memory of dead bodies.

At night, the people of the projects' lyrical voices are mixed with laughter at the latest joke. There is a quizzical lightness and some people, usually at the ends of the benches, try to explain the meaning of the black-and-white print in newspapers. There are dim lights in almost every window of the projects. The government is paying for the electricity, so why not let the light shine, illuminating rooms with sparse furniture, drying clothes and children with a thousand questions.

All of that would be gone, replaced by dark houses where no one seems to work and everyone has red eyes, especially the parents.

The next morning, I am up early, and I can hear my mother rumbling downstairs. Before I'm fully downstairs, I can see the boxes and smell the torn paper and frantic activity.

"Ma, what in heck are you doing?"

"Moving. Like I told you. We have to get the hell out of here."

"Why?"

"Why you think? Niggers shooting dope out in the open, breaking into apartments and killing each other like red ants and you ask me why in the hell we have to move?"

"But there are good people here."

"I know but they are few and far between and they're getting plucked off by a bullet with no name on it."

"So, are you trying to run?"

"No, son, just hide. Until you can graduate from high school and get prepared to hit those bricks."

"What the hell does that mean?"

"I have to protect you from these niggers until I can get you in a college and then we can both get out of here."

"You hate it here that much?"

"It's not where I want to die."

"But if you don't want to die, then why don't you stop drinking, Ma? Alcohol is killing you quicker than anything."

"Now, you into grown folks' business."

"But, Ma, I'm worried about you. Really."

"Don't be. I can handle my own misery."

"That's just it. It doesn't have to be miserable all the time."

"Thank you for teaching me, son, but I have my own history book to carry."

The kitchen seems to be getting darker. It is all too overwhelming, but I need to find some way of articulating what I see every day, trying to understand it all myself. The most important thing is to find a way to get your head bad, especially on Friday and Saturday nights, to forget everything around you. On the weekends, the people of South Jamaica try to crawl in cracks between the walls and linoleum floors quick with roaches. My mother's face is a wall. I go back to my room and try to wonder.

I pull out the journal of what I used to be.

January 1967
Today is a monumental day. I scored fifty-seven points last night
in a rec center league game. Twenty-one points in one quarter, with seven-minute running time. The ball just floated off my hands and into the bottom of the net. It didn't even feel like playing; it felt like dancing on the hardwood. People came out of their houses and up to the gym just to watch the game. I don't know if I will ever feel this way again. Things were so fluid, it was like everything was passing by my eyes in a flashback from a movie.

I can hear my mother stumbling downstairs. She hides the bottle behind the refrigerator and takes the drink out when she thinks I'm sleeping. That's when she really ties one on but each night, I can hear her footsteps and I know that she has reached that point, where she will simply pour it down with no feeling or pretense of taste. It is like a poison elixir to her and each night she puts more and more on the emotional wound of my father leaving, but the alcohol does not heal or make the open, wound close. Alcohol never seems to make people happy—it takes your looks, health, ruins your relationships and makes you not care about how you appear, and then alcohol wants more: your living life. It wants every aspect of optimism destroyed and with each bottom of the bottle, my mother is helping the drug succeed. Shriveling like a sponge that has been used too long. The lines on her face become more pronounced and she looks like a dried-out prune. I am watching her die in front of me, slowly, and there ain't a damn thing I can do about it. She will have to see her own self in the mirror.

I am up early the next morning, out on the block. Each morning there are stories about who got shot last; they wind and move on the early winds of day. This morning the rumors are different.

Miss Catherine, Sandra's mom, is the mother of the neighborhood and her house is a gathering place. Long legs dangle from the edge of the couch. As I head downstairs, on the stairs outside of Catherine's house, leading to the front door of the community center, Catherine calls out to me.
 "Richard, have you heard…"
 "Heard what…"
 "About William. He got the letter. He's going."
 "Going where…?"
 "To the Nam. Vietnam."
 "When did he get the letter?"
 "Last night."

"Damn."

My lottery number is 256 and William's was 217. I know that these numbers represent thousands of boys that are going to a certain death, and I know that mine may be coming up soon. Each night, I watch Walter Cronkite and check the number of kills of the enemy that America tells us about. If you listen to the news, it seems like we're winning the war. I know different—my friends who do not come back in pine boxes tell me the real deal. The North Vietnamese have fighting techniques we have never seen before. They're dropping out of trees, creating booby traps and planting mines all over the damn place. My friends come back with sleeves and pants-legs waving in the wind. Everything has been blown off, disturbed, or destroyed. And the neighborhood is devoid of men; there are women holding the hands of fatherless children or about to be fatherless children. There are no complete families as far as I can see. Vietnam has ripped South Jamaica apart.

I move slowly up the block toward Jamaica Avenue, seeing outlines only, no actual people. It is like we are all traveling with the ghost of Vietnam on our shoulders. There is a feeling of loss is in the atmosphere, and it seems like the air is drained of life and possibility. Something feels tinny and hollow, almost like a lot with abandoned cars. The hum of conversation is gone and there is a flat feeling surrounding me. The war is taking all the men. We miss their booming voices and laughter away from the squares where people sit on benches that face each other. The top of the projects seems to have been taken off.

But, about a half a mile away, Jamaica Avenue is buzzing with life. The foreign vendors stand proudly next to their oranges and fruits at the stands. They have a look of ownership on their faces as I move between them, squeezing my way to the subway. Sometimes, I pause, just as I'm approaching Archer Avenue and look back down the hill at the people that appear like ants, or Sisyphus rolling the ball with his nose that will inevitably come back down, falling to 109th Avenue and 160th Street.

The subway is jammed today. I didn't notice but it is a Monday morning. That means there will be hundreds of businessmen sitting with their folded *New York Times* in rider's faces. I want to ball up their papers and throw them back at them. They are too self-absorbed and too satisfied—their business is the only business.

The air conditioning is on, and I stand, strap hanging. I'm going to the employment office today to try to get a job, but I don't really want one. Twenty-two-year-olds that have just graduated from college are the prime targets of the midget man named Nixon.

When I get to the 42nd Street station, I come up from the underground and find a table at a vest pocket park. I have my journal with me now; it has become required reading.
    I stop at the Donnell Library on 53rd Street to read my journal.

1961

    Today was a groovy day. My mother and I stood on a long line in sub-freezing temperatures to see this sculpture by Michelangelo called the PIETÀ. I complained

for hours. "Why in the heck do we have to see this?
What's so important about this sculpture? We could
have been in the Museum of Modern Art seven times
by now. That's my hangout. The twentieth century,
and not this old stuff. What is so important about this sculpture?"
"You'll see, son," is all she said. I
grew tired of standing and my legs felt like they
would melt into the concrete. But, once inside,
when the line shortened, I could see the reason
for the wait.

She shined. Much more brilliant
than anything I could ever see. The marble
is luminescent and I am amazed by the look of
the Virgin Mary as she holds the baby Jesus in
her arms. She looks like the mothers I have
seen in Baisley Park. There are people behind me
but I don't want to move. I am mesmerized by
the lines and the eyes of this beautiful work of art.

For the first time this week, I make it downtown, alone. The employment office is full of "deplorables". I don't fit in with these baggy-pants old men and perky, hopeful women with resumés and energy. I don't know what field to go into or what line to stand on. I just don't want to go to Vietnam, and I need to help my mother as much as I can if I go. I look for the appropriate sign. Maybe I'll start with the secretary.

"Excuse me, can you tell me where I would go for employment services?"

I find the "unemployment office" on the second floor. When I find a cold, plastic seat, I start to read my journal again, which I carry with me.

December 1961

This morning we braved the cold again to stand in a line outside of the Metropolitan Museum of Art. The Museum is near the stone walls of Central Park and the tall gray buildings bounce the cold wind back to you. The lady in front of me is complaining out loud. "The Mona Lisa... you used to tell me I was your Mona Lisa."
Once inside, the line is longer. At the end of the line, there is a small, dark booth with the shades half drawn. A single golden light shines above what I perceive to be a face. I move up slowly and as I do, the expression on the face seems to change from a smirk to a mysterious, enigmatic smile. There is nothing behind Mona Lisa accept some countryside and I move to the painting one step at a time, careful not to rush to the light, to the imperfect perfection of her face. But there is a power, a light within, that becomes a little like metal, drawing me. I move a little closer to the contents of the curtain and the brighter light there within. There is some countryside behind her, maybe a tree or two. But that is all lost as I concentrate on her forehead, her lips. The smile is not puzzling, it is compelling, and as the gray-haired lady in front of me moves upward toward the dim light—the lips compel and challenge me to come into her aura, and I move

like a child accepting baptism.
Mona Lisa's face takes me in and pushes me back at the same time. It is not simply beauty, her look seems to be the origin of things beatific and wonderful. Once I stand in front of her, I want to cower, to find a space to crawl into. **I am not worthy of the calm in her eyes and the promised universes within her.**

Because we left museum early, we are in the first third of the line. We zoomed into Manhattan quickly, the F train is running efficiently, as tourists with hopeful smiles imagine what Radio City Music Hall and the Rockettes' legs will look like, sparkling on the huge, dark stage of Radio City. I walk to 57th Street. The Museum of Modern Art is more than a city block. I love the vine covered buildings and solid stone. The line, to see the sculpture stretches blocks now, as people with shapeless clothing blend in with the perfect brick walls of the Hayden Planetarium. I look behind me and all I can see are the tops of heads. People shuffle their legs with anticipation; there is a cross section of humanity—squiggling kids half-holding their parents' hands, older people waiting to see beauty distilled and jumpy teenagers insistent and resentful, like I was before I saw her.

That was years ago, and I wish I could go back to that time but there are different concerns now; that plague me as I am standing here; the next line I stand in may mean my life.

I am fighting off demands from the American Government to see a different kind of hillside. I might even have to find a job, or something. I have been floating ever since they gave me a high school diploma. There is nothing in New York City but college or the life of the wealthy child with the planned existence.

I have no planned existence, so I wander around, trying to avoid my mother's screams and the nothingness of the alleyway. Finding a job in the most competitive city in the world is not easy. Everyone has degrees and suits with lapels-that-do-not-move. and they speak with university tones.

I feel more comfortable around the dropouts of Manhattan society—the ones with dark circles under their eyes, the unemployed. The older men have baggy clothing that ring like bells on their malnourished legs. The women are intimidating with their perfectly manicured resumés and pressed business suits. I am waiting on the line for people with only high school diplomas. It moves slowly.

"Fill out this form fully, sir, without deleting any of the spaces and bring that back to me."

When I get back home, Ma is hugging boxes with tape. Her hands are moving with quick anger. She wants me to be excited about the move, but I don't feel anything but a small hammer hitting in my chest.

"You're going to have to clean out your own room."
"I know that."
"But you need to do it soon."
"Why…?"
"The movers will be here next Wednesday. This time I got some professionals."
"Okay, I'll start."

My shoulders hunch as I head upstairs to try to make sense out of the piles of dark clothing and scattered papers. I really don't have much that I want to keep, but there is a lot to throw away. There will be no more late nights looking at Sandra's curves through the venetian blinds, so I better enjoy my last evenings of living on the square, on the second floor, just above four benches where people party. I go to my bedroom window to check; I call Sandra.

She agrees to dance behind the yellow, torn venetian blinds one more time. I go outside and stand in the grass, to watch her window. I can barely see her move, her body is like a violin; then she undulates and shakes for me, and I can circumscribe her shadow in my brain, as she dips three times then comes back up, spreading her arms against the yellow light of her bedroom. She touches the window for a minute and then she turns around, twisting and gyrating until I can barely think. I can smell the dark lilacs of her thighs from here; my fingers tingle to touch her raw silk skin.

I throw some things in sloppy boxes that the movers will have trouble with.

The next day I'm supposed to meet Sandra, near her broken-down school—Performing Arts High School that should have been torn down a long time ago. It looks like an old, dilapidated castle falling in on itself. The gray bricks have lost their life a long time ago and barely hold up the structure. Performing Arts High School was built in 1947 with big ugly brick and foggy windows are repelling. It is a dirty little cave where all of life opens onstage.

I didn't really tell Sandra I was coming to get her—I like to surprise her and her snooty friends sometimes by just showing up. Sandra acts like her nose is perpendicular to the ground and that her dancer friends are somehow better than me or going to turn out better—other times she's regular.

She's waiting at the end of the block, standing alone, with her tights hanging off her arms. *Will wonders never fucking cease? She's on time.* Her light-brown eyes seem to have a fleck of sunshine red in them. The sun is starting to climb into the envelope of carbon monoxide darkness. Sandra seems almost happy to see me.

"Did you have a fight with your friends?"

"No, I figured I'd just be waiting for you this time, make it easy on you."

"Since when did that start to happen?"

"What do you mean?"

"You're making it easy for me."

"Call it a new program."

Sandra's face was beaming for some reason. There was a kind of internal glow that I had never seen before.

"Yeah, if you say so." I take her hand and we walk a little faster to the subway.

"What's your rush?"

"I mean, people are always rushing in the city, I guess it just becomes a habit."

"I like to look at everyone coming and going sometimes, like ants."

She pulls me down to a stone bench near a fountain in front of a huge building on Sixth Avenue.

"Look at them. Every one of them is on a mission."

"Too intense."

"I love it."

"But you're a dancer—you love the stage and the music and the speed and all of that."

"I guess I do. The beat is sort of in my blood."

"I like it in Queens."

"Too slow for me. My heart moves to the beat of Manhattan. Duke Ellington baby."

Sandra sleeps on my shoulder all the way home. Her dance shoes are dirty, and she is breathing like a truck driver. Her feet look battered and worn—her bunions are dusty, and the bottoms are black. Sandra is breathing deeply, sleeping.

I just stare at the lady across from me, with the curving calves and sheer black stockings. She seems to open her legs when the train rocks, staring at me as I try to find light between her shapely thighs. By the time we get out to Queens, Sandra is slobbering on my shoulder. She has been sound asleep, on the rocking train, for a solid hour. I am hungry as hell.

"Wake up. Sandra, wake the fuck up. We're here."

I drag her up and out before the bell and the closing of the subway doors. Parsons Boulevard is full of clumps of people that just stand. Multiple accents and languages assault the air.

"Damn. I was tired as hell. Those dance teachers think we're professionals."

"Well, as long as you been dancing, and the way you dance, people would think you are a professional."

"Was that a compliment?"

"Sort of, I mean I don't get the whole dance thing at all but the people clap, and what you're doing looks impressive, and you're flexible as hell. I can attest to that."

"Thanks for the recommendation. I didn't know you cared

or concentrated enough on what I'm doing to make a comment."

The New York Boulevard bus is a dark hovel. Somebody lets Sandra sit down.

"Thank you. She needs it."

"Thank you."

Sandra slumps in the chair, still wearing her day on her downturned face. Sleep will come soon. I wake her up when we get to our stop, and she bumps down the stairs while I hold her under her arms.

We both bend as we take the shortcut through the fence at 40 Park, Sandra holds my hand and tries to avoid the pieces of glass as I look at her calves shake back and forth between the shards.

"Are you coming over tonight?"

"To watch you sleep…?"

"Come over tomorrow night. If it's real late, knock on the window."

Sandra lives on the second floor; I can get in by catching the jutted, slate ledge of the window with my fingers, as she opens the window, as I pull myself into the muted light of her room. It is like leaping into a universe of Aretha Franklin with the touch of purple satin. Her room has pristine, white furniture with gold trim. It looks like a room for a project princess. I don't knock and catch her turning into the hind pocket of sleep. I watch her for a moment, moving over on her pillow. I leave before her mother discovers me.

Once in my building, I climb up the dark steps, thinking of Sandra's gowns.

Mom is downstairs, making a racket again. I guess she is serious about moving. At least that makes one of us. There is a small opening, at the bottom of the huge window in my room. From out of this small glass vent, I can see Sandra's window and the rectangles and circles of the stone playground in the back of my building. Sometimes kids crawl to the top of the monkey bars and sometimes the park is a sculpture of chipped concrete and faded color. From this rectangle, I see the world. It is a small space, but from this window I can view the playground, the three-story buildings that seem to grow out of trees and the bathroom window of Sandra. That's all I need to see.

The next morning the house is full of strange people—movers—grabbing boxes and heading out the door to the dark house. I've only been there once, and it seems spooky and too large to me. How will we fill up those rooms, just my mother and me? I wish my father were here with his booming voice. His voice would fill the rooms and his rumbling was like mine. I guess, in a sneaky way, he affirmed me, and I reflected him.

But the bottles all around the house and the redness in my mother's eyes did not allow her to see him. It was not just his presence, but my father had a quick and aggressive mind—he was always reading the *New York Times* or some book with a title I could barely pronounce. He tried to talk to my mother about big things, philosophical things, but she wanted him to concentrate on cleaning the house, washing the kitchen floors, and getting a second job. Dad always worked, eight, nine, sometimes ten hours a day at the post office, but when he came home, he wanted to play the trumpet.

He would go up to the roof or outside in the cold, in the square, with his hands shaking, holding up sheet music, intermittently putting his fingers in the trumpet case for warmth, and then he would send beautiful, melodic messages over the tenements, into the air. It was like he spoke through the circles and rim of his horn. I could always tell his mood by the music he made. If he was in a good mood, it was Miles Davis, with the mute in his horn. If he was feeling bad, the horn would sound brassy, with a hot edge to it. An angry and abrasive Dizzy Gillespie. My dad made the air bearable because of his notes.

I don't think Mom ever really listened to his playing, but I did, every night. It made the pop-pop of gun shots bearable. Mom only made fun of him when he came inside.

"What do you think… you're going to make it to Carnegie Hall… What in the hell are you playing that twisted up, battered thing for? I can't spend those tunes. I need some cash. Something I can spend at the convenience store. I can't spend that avant-garde jazz shit you play. Ain't even got no rhythm. Like niggers or White people for that matter, want to hear that. Not even those weird wiggers with the stringy hair want to hear that shit. You ain't worth a damn."

I guess he got tired of hearing it.

She is brittle and I'm starting to realize it doesn't have a damn thing to do with me. I wish I could rewind the film of my family and go back to a former frame but that doesn't seem to be happening. My mother talks down to me, but she seems to be speaking to the bottle that she would like to crawl out of.

I guess, after struggling with this so long, she has decided that there is nothing to do but be angry, but anger takes her deeper into her personal prison. As she makes love to bottle after bottle, she seems to be more and more upset with her need to get to the bottom of each one. She is knocking at the walls of her self-inflicted cell, yelling at everyone around her. Her favorite target is my father. Their voices come up through the floor like saws.

"You really think that bottle will help get you out of these projects, and away from all of us?"

"I don't want to be away from my boy, but you have to admit you jump in my shit and smash it in my face every day."

"That's because it stinks. It stinks when you're sleeping and when you're awake. Do you feel like a consummate failure, because you are… your own child doesn't give a tinker's damn about you and we have virtually no relationship because whenever I want to talk sweet to you, you're picking up that battered horn and pressing your lips against her."

"Now, you must be the first woman to be jealous of a damn instrument. Now, come on. You got to be able to do better than that."

"I can't reach you. Your brain is always occupied."

"Is there anything wrong with that? An empty mind is a devil's fucking workshop."

"But don't you ever want to talk about what I want to talk about?"

"Which is what… Mrs. Marvelyn didn't do her hair or who is next for the corner or the grave? How can you talk so much about nothing?"

"All you want to do is talk heavy, existentialism up and jazz down."

"That's what I like, philosophy and music. Why does that offend you so?"

"Anything that takes you away from me offends me."

"Oh, so now we get to the crux. You want to control what I do every hour of the freaking day."

"Not really."

"Since I work twelve hours sometimes and only have a few

hours before I go to sleep—then you want to control my free time, that only time of the day I have to myself before I crawl in the sack. That's when I am most myself and you want to take that the fuck away from me?"

"Not really, I just want you to be present when you're at home."

"That shit sounds really good but what it comes down to is this—I want a life beyond the everyday and you want to snatch that away from me, like it subtracts from your life for me to have some enjoyment in mine."

"Not really. You're twisting things all around."

"No, I just see through your little domestic façade. Harmony really means control. You're not happy unless you're pulling my strings like I'm a pre-civil war marionette."

"I just need an all-the-time man, not a sometime man."

Journal entry, 1963

> They are downstairs dissecting each other again. I can hear their words come through the floor. At first, they used to discuss, then debate—tonight they're just yelling at the top of their lungs. How can they hear each other if they yell? I wish I could squeeze out of the bottom window and jump from monkey bar to monkey bar on my way up. In my daydreams I am at the top of the monkey bars, like a champion, where only Wee Willie, William Waters sits because he is faster than everyone else; he swings his legs like an Olympic champion. It's a totally different world up there—at the top of the monkey bars, where no one can touch me. All the dead junkies that I see every day while walking to school dry up and disappear.

My parents are still yelling at each other downstairs.

"What in the hell did you get married for anyway woman?"

"You got married to get out of your mother's house. I was a convenient ploy. You even hid how crazy she was from me because you knew if I truly peeped it, I would run for the first available hill."

"Well, we're here now and we might as well make the most of it."

"I think we are long past that. You won't accept me as an artist."

"But you're not an artist. You're a stevedore. You work on the railroad, and you pick up the White man's bags. You ain't nothing but Tom to him. "Tom, get my bags. Tom, would you help my daughter with her doll—Tom.' Nothing but an Uncle Tom."

"That's some nasty shit and you know it."

"But you ain't no Miles fucking Davis. Your ass can't even read music."

"A lot of great musicians can't read music. You got to feel it and when you feel it in your spine, then you know you're a musician."

"Well, I can't feel that. I don't know what the fuck you're talking about."

"That's what I mean. Could you try to feel it? That's why we're so far apart—you don't want to feel what I feel, and I don't know what you feel."

"Numb."

"Is that it…?"

"Except when I'm drinking. That's the only time I feel

things—but it doesn't last. It moves quickly through me and out, like a piece of shit."

"Does the drinking help you feel?'

"No, it helps me not feel and because we have this chasm between us, drinking is the best deal downstairs."

"Yeah, and what I'm proposing is that we go upstairs a little bit and think some higher thoughts instead of being wrapped up in every day. I feel like I'm tied to the kitchen floor and the kitchen floor is the tip of the earth and if I fall, I'll fall into some space."

"Blackness. Now, we're talking. That's the space I want to fall into. That's why I crack that seal on that vodka bottle."

"And does it work for you?"

"Sometimes, when I can get enough to drink. My hope is to get to oblivion every night."

"And where is that…?"

"Just before I black out, there are specks; maybe they're things I'm hallucinating, and those little specks become lights that seem to hurt my eyes after a time. And then the pain comes, from not enough water in my system or maybe my liver is giving way, but there's a sharp pain in my back that moves to my stomach and then I can hear you or Richard upstairs, but its faint, like I'm not really here and moving to a new place, a new world where everything is black and it affirms me for a second before I fall out."

"That's one of the saddest stories I've ever heard."

And so, it was. Almost every night I would hear them, for hours, and after my father left there was silence. I missed his man-ness, his form and breathing as he walks through the house, but I do enjoy going to sleep to the sweet sound of gunshots and screaming for dope instead of two people going at each other—

trying to get what the other one does not have. That is the worst of all, to hear grating, desperate, angry voices like blades of knives, clashing.

I know that sounds crazy, but in the projects, after nine or ten, the war begins for turf and women and dope. I'm used to the sounds of the brick buildings, with gunshots punctuating the night. I am even used to the final shot, bass, crackling like a crematorium fire proclaiming a life.

I do not want to leave what I have become accustomed to, for the dark houses and empty mysteries of Union Hall Street. I don't know what they talk about over there, what they do over in those private houses—I like the smallness of an apartment; sharing a wall with another family is like sharing a life. You know about their pain because you can hear it, and their death because you can see it. Besides, my mother doesn't understand that I enjoy the community of the vest pocket park.

Sometimes, the girlfriends sitting at the end of the bench, in the vest pocket squares between project buildings, will ask me to write a letter to their "men" in Indochina; most of the girls can't write a sentence, let alone a paragraph. The squares, between the buildings are the places where I hang and receive information. I love the wood slats of the benches and the loud talk into the skinny hours of powder-blue mornings rising over six-story roofs.

Once home, the clanging of glass to ice to liquor makes me shudder. I would rather hear voices.

Our new house on Union Hall Street, is intimidating, dark and I live on the second floor. My new room yawns with aching nothingness. There is nothing there—no furniture yet. Ma has asked me about what I want but I can't think of anything. I just feel heavy—like I want to find some place in the house to crawl under. I look for a crack in the baseboards.

Journal entry: January 1967
    Ever since I was about twelve, I've had this feeling.
It starts in my lower stomach and then grows, like
it's owning my body. It kind of feels like heat but
I know it's not just the heat. Now, today, it is taking me
over. I feel like I'm under water and like it was at
camp, I'm a non-swimmer that cannot come above. I am
barely breathing sometimes. I just walk around the
house and look at the emptiness of the rooms.
I think about what might happen here and everything
is bad. The dark rooms have owned my imagination
and I see few playgrounds or benches
where people gather. They have sheets up at the
windows because they can't afford curtains. The
residents of Union Hall Street say that they are
better than the people of the projects. The first
day somebody called me a "nigger from over there
in the forty projects." That made me turn around
and want to fucking strangle them. I have been
in my room for two days, walking from window
to window. I feel like a vice has my nuts. There is
no one on the streets here—
I know Mike Kennedy and a few others that
live here, near my new home, on Union Hall Street, but
they hide in the house and catch
needles in the crook of their arms, thinking they
are more high class than the junkies in the projects.
These niggers are less than those niggers over there.
At least in the projects, people are for real. Today
I must get out the house. Sandra said she might

be free tonight but right now I just need to walk down the fucking street and get some fucking air.

I pass the empty lots and abandoned cars every day, but today I see them clearly.

The air rushes down my lungs and I stare right and left. Aside from the bilious houses, there are empty lots with abandoned cars all up and down street. They are hidden by corrugated iron fences that have holes in them or lean to one side, showing the battered cars with missing batteries and frames without doors. There are at least three of these abandoned car lots on the street. There is a dead silence.

South Road leads to the infamous "Bucket of Blood" bar. Dead bodies have been thrown through the half doors and there is sand on the floor; blues music floats from the jukebox to the air every late night. Once, I went in, in the morning—the tables were being washed down and the floor was being swept. It was as calm as a church but at night, blades unfurl, and punctured bodies are thrown out of the swinging wood slat doors.

No one seems to come to these vacant lots on Union Hall Street and I am not sure of how they sell their car parts. Everything is done in secret on this street. No one stands on the corner and laughs—everyone whispers behind their hands, setting up drug deals to be played out later.

Sandra is late and I sit on her couch, covered with plastic slipcovers, waiting, discussing the latest overdose in the projects with her mother.

"Yeah, Miss Catherine, this heroin thing is a scourge."

"It will take a tall, proud young man and make him a shell of himself in a month, with that crazy look in their eyes, always borrowing money from you."

"And they act like it's something they have to chase."

"Like you are chasing my daughter. Just joking, it's worse than that. They act like this drug is giving them something. Between that and Vietnam, we won't have a man left."

"All I see is young girls pushing baby carriages."

CHAPTER TWO

I waited for Sandra until seven o'clock. Every night, at seven, there is only one activity for me—watching the nightly news. Nothing is at it appears—and everything has a double or triple fucking meaning. No one is sure of anything because war can eradicate good, and even though we have posters that promote saving "plants and other living things," America is stumbling, according to the ant-war movement and the students on the campus of Columbia University, in Harlem, America is becoming more autocratic.

Everyone says Columbia is in upper Manhattan, but it stretches to sho' nuff Harlem. The Students for a Democratic Society are some serious people.

We don't know if we're sharing a joint with a brother or an F.B.I. man. Everyone in the country seems to be turning, and veterans are demonstrating against the war.

We are not what we once were in the eyes of the world and the nightly news shows American's growing discontent with dropping bombs on Laos and Vietnam. The domino theory is falling, making a thud.

The war comes into our living room every night and so do the rationales from Washington; this is like living in an Otto Preminger movie. I feel like I'm in the twilight zone all the time—people talk to you one day and then they become air, lost in the mist and myth of Vietnam.

Lyndon Baines Johnson is a confused man and each night

his face tells a different story than his words. There is something good in the deceitful, hound dog look of Lyndon Baines Johnson but there is something even better in the calm and peaceful delivery of Walter Cronkite. Even though he is a White man, there is an element of his personality that I trust. Maybe it was when he took his glasses off and wiped his eyes after John Fitzgerald Kennedy was shot.

The war seems to be weighing on Walter Cronkite as each night he gives the trumped-up figures of how many American boys have died and how many North Vietnamese. I distrust these figures, because to me, we want to keep the myth alive, the myth of America never losing a war. Tonight, Walter Cronkite says, on the CBS evening news, "we are at a stalemate."

It is getting toward the end of the show, and I am sitting at the edge of the bed. I can hear the faint gunshots of early evening coming from the park in the back of the house. As the night wears on, the shots become more pronounced, closer—they seem to start over in the park and move toward the building as victims run.

"The lottery numbers for the evening are…" and this means thousands of boys with these numbers will be called into the service—the lottery numbers for the evening are… 215–235. All able-bodied males between the ages of eighteen and twenty-seven should report immediately to their local conscription office."

I didn't hear it. My number is 256 and I know the next time this fatherly man takes the air, he may be calling my number and punching my plane ticket at the same time.

Sandra says she's going to Central Park with me this Saturday. I'm supposed to pick her up at one, but I always have to wait for her to dress, put on the proper shoes and get her colors coordinated.

I knock on the iron door and the peephole swings open.

"I'm ready."

And she is—shorts and sandals.

"What's wrong with you?"

"Nothing."

"Come on, now, don't lie to your girl."

"Are you my girl, really?"

"I thought I was, unless you have somebody else."

"Well, how come I never see you?"

"Dance has me. Dance is my boyfriend if you want to think of it that way."

"I know something is pulling you away from me."

By the time we get to the subway, the conversation has stilled. There is enough tension and sadness to cut the thick subway air with a butter knife.

"What's wrong, Richard…? You're as moody as a pregnant woman."

"My lottery number for Vietnam is close. Walter might announce it next week some time."

"Walter?"

"Walter Cronkite, the newscaster."

"You act like you know him."

"I feel like I do. He's kind of fatherly and he comes into my room every night by way of television."

"Do you miss your dad?"

"Yeah, but the way my mother is hitting that bottle, I would have left too."

"So, you do miss him?"

"Yeah, but there's something about Walter Cronkite, something fatherly. I mean, I know he's a White man but there's something teddy bear like about him."

"Okay, I can't see it, but if you say so."

"And last night Walter Cronkite went up to 235, and I'm number 256—they'll be calling my number soon."

The lights of the subway flash on and off; as they do, Sandra hugs me by my waist, tight like she has never done before. We say nothing until we change to the D train at 42nd Street. She leans on my shoulder and goes to sleep on the leather arm of my blue and white Tech jacket.

"If you go, they'll probably put you on a hill with a gun and you'll sit there and have orders to shoot but nobody will ever come near you."

"You got it all worked out, huh?"

"I love you, Richard."

We exit at 59th Street Columbus Circle and begin to immediately search for a rock in Central Park. I find my favorite—the one with four or five different surfaces and levels. I pull Sandra up and sit like a king on his changing throne. Each time I come to Central Park, there is different graffiti, names immortalized on the park benches.

Chi Chi 1967 Rhonda and Susan forever.
Big baller 68.

The train ride home seems like a short one because Sandra is enfolded within my arms.

I go over to visit Sandra, like I do every night, and she makes me wait in her room. She disappears to the bathroom. I wait on her small cot, listening to the sounds of the neighborhood.

The telephone cable/jump ropes are being put away—I hear the final scraping on the concrete and the girls' voices discuss who will be the first ones to turn the cables of "double-dutch" in the morning.

I doze and just when I'm about to put my head on the concrete, she comes in. Resplendent in purple, flowing and frilly.

"Damn."

"Give you something to think about when you're away."

"Away—you already got plans with someone else…"

"No, I just meant—"

"I know what you meant…"

I turn away from her and look out of the window.

"I'm going to Union Hall Street."

Sandra and I don't see each other for about a week. It's seven o'clock and Walter Cronkite is on again with more news from the front. He hesitates and moves his papers with trepidation and slowness. It's almost like he does not want to read what he must.

"Numbers 235–267" is all I heard.

The induction center is crowded and stinking of cigarette smoke and old alcohol. We are given a battery of tests to determine intelligence, problem solving skills and the ability to adapt to your environment. Everyone looks scared or stoned or both. Some are screaming and acting crazy—they're put on the bus first. I am standing behind a skinny white guy with a dirty T-shirt. Most of the Whites are sent to the right; for some reason they send me to the right also.

"This is the line for the Army and if you would have gone left, you would have ended up who knows where. Sorry-sacks, consider yourselves lucky. You will become part of the elite fighting-machine known as the United States Army. We are leading the war against those gooks and wiping them out as quickly as the sun shines and now you will be involved in the war to save Democracy and to keep those dirty Viet Cong from infecting Laos and Cambodia with their communist shit and you will be fighting alongside Marines and other brothers to win this fucking war!

"By stepping forward you are accepting enlistment in the defense of the government of the United States…"

That's all I remember hearing.

We were given forty-five days to put our affairs in order, but I don't have any affairs but Sandra. I must make sure that she will be there waiting for me when I return. I know niggers got their eyes peeled like freshly cut potatoes, watching, and waiting for me to leave so they can pounce on Sandra. I must fight down the fear.

Something in me died the minute I received the letter from the local draft board. It wasn't that I wasn't expecting it—it just made it all final for me. An official letter from the American government. It is a notice to go and fight and kill brown people and die for the same nation that put my people in slavery for 250 years. The letter has raised print and a government seal, but I start crying and drop the damn thing on the linoleum floor, right after I read it.

They have never written me before and the first letter I

receive asks me to give up my life. Now, many in the neighborhood go without question; they did not believe they had the right to object or protest. It was too late for me though—there was no getting out of it now, not flat feet or the last son or any of that. All of that have been waived—it was too late to create an illness or mental problems; I had to go.

I knew that the open windows of the projects would be gone for me forever; the entire landscape around me would be changing. Whenever they call the numbers, thousands of boys must go. It seems like all the men are being sucked through the windows of the projects into a huge vacuum called the 'Nam. Not only have my friends come back with pieces of them missing and with crutches and prostheses, but there is life gone in their eyes when they come back. It is almost like everything that they had seen before, all the light and color and beauty of the world was pushed out and I catch them, in the middle of the afternoon, staring into vacancies, boring a hole in the sky with their looks.

And each time I see them, the look gets deeper, more intense and they would seem go to that canyon of grief every day. It was almost like if I shot off a gun in their face, they wouldn't hear it. It seems like they visit old pictures in their minds, again and again. There was something deep, swallowing them the fuck up and I could not figure it was. Sometimes, weeks after seeing them with the numb look on their faces, I would catch the same look on the cats hanging out on New York Boulevard, standing on the corner, waiting, for their own destruction to visit them. It wasn't Vietnam but the internal war of self-destruction they were fighting and losing.

They all seem to be waiting for a bus that will never arrive. The young men on New York Boulevard are stuck in the worst mental cement. First, you see them sucking the end of twisted paper, then they will be huddled up in the corner with their cronies, sniffing something out of a glassine bag and finally the forty-five degrees, where they would lean at forty-five degrees, eyes closed, in a mouth-turned-down-nod and not fall smack dab on the block, from their angle; immediately, when they come down from their all-consuming high, they begin to distrust all squares. Everyone that doesn't stick a needle in their arm is seen as a square, an enemy to their suicidal universe. There are no flowers in their gardens anymore and plants do not sprout their heads out of project soil.

The old ladies had planted gardens, using their Alabama and Mississippi knowledge of the land, but all of that has been torn up. There is nothing but clumps of men, with lines surrounding where their eyes used to be. There are only empty shadows, that men used to cast. When you catch the homeboys nodding, dope-sick in the morning, then you know they are intent on dying. A man with nothing to lose is as dangerous as a flung knife on the next stairwell. One by one, I could almost predict where my friends were on the cycle of self-destruction. They look like they are in the woods, once holding the hand of Robert Frost, but he has let go, and now they are lost.

The nodding from the heaviness of heroin is a sure sign that they are fading, giving themselves up to the emptiness between the buildings and the pool halls—few will make it back. Weeks later, after the first appearance of road tracks, their eyes will be sliding out of their heads, complete with broken blood vessels, yellow teeth, and a sallow look of dehydration. The life the drug has taken from them; everything is drawing up in the needle with the heroin and then we just wait, in front of our project buildings, for the news. In months or sometimes days it will come—with just their name and the headline: "Jimmy Mack, former basketball star, O.D."

A broken-off part inside of me will feel good, that the misery and looks of blank tomorrows in their eyes are gone. Jimmy Mack, who was my arch opponent at Forest Hills High school died this morning.

When the narratives started to swirl about his addiction—it hit me. He was so fast and self-assured on the court, he seemed invincible. Jimmy Mack no longer had to stare out of the window for hours.

A cavern in my stomach would start to tense up with each new tale of someone here yesterday and gone today, a new story that is attached to each new death, each character, the pristine descriptions of the nights when they passed away, makes my muscles quiver and they will not release.

It is that same empty cavern of feeling that came over me the moment Walter Cronkite betrayed me and called out my number. It was a deep funk that I couldn't get off me for days and days—like a linebacker that you're unable to shake. My head is pointed downward and there's no way I can turn it up. And then this futility gets inside me, like gas, and I know there is nothing I can do.

This feeling of death crawling within my body, after getting this fucking letter from Tricky Dick is much worse than waiting to be shot by some nigger around the corner. I feel the emotional weight every day, like an anvil, in my chest. Going to Viet Nam is like being a sacrificial lamb for America. They never wrote me a letter before. And the deep funk of this death sentence on my back stays with me. I seldom go outside but I know I must force myself to open the front door. I play Isaac Hayes' *Hot Buttered Soul,* until the grooves have grooves.

By the time I get to Phoenix…

Eventually, I open the front door, but I am afraid of the wind of every day. It is difficult. Every day, staying behind the door makes living more complex; my hand starts to shake when I approach the knob.

One night, after listening to music all day, I decide to go downtown and just walk around, to see what I am missing.

Forty-second Street can depress you or it can excite. There are lots of lights, and places where you can get lost in booths where girls open their legs and show what their mothers told them not to. The billboards of each movie house promise live sex shows.

This makes me feel dirty and worse than I did a few minutes ago. I walk fast past the soiled neon lights, to the stretch limos and French women with servants and long legs that seem to go on forever.

I look across the street and play the city game I used to play, of racing someone I don't know. The gray ghost of what looms soon, is still in front of me, laughing. He is the figure of a skinny White man in uniform without any medals that I can see. When I think of going to Vietnam, he is what I think of.

Vietnam is the place where people go to die. I can't lose my life in the rice paddies. Mental diversion is the key. In New York City, with its rushing crowds, and throngs of people, there is much to capture the eye. I've got to think of something other than Vietnam, the bunker and the rats and leeches that will share my home underground.

I look across the street and find my racing victim. In a city of 8.5 million, you must make up games to survive. One game I have created for myself is to race someone down the block who is unaware, on the other side of the street. I pick out my victim. He is a tall man, with a crumpled suit and a look that seems to say, "I need to get home," on his face. It is the frantic, pressed in look of the dehydrated New Yorker that has been beaten up by the day and has nothing left.

I look down at his legs and check his pace. It is a normal pace, but he speeds up to get around people. He looks like he is trying to make an appointment. I have no dates or appointments, but I pick up the speed with him and when he avoids people, I do too. The key to walking in New York City is to anticipate—it is like driving; the walker must identify the visitors from Iowa who will stop in the middle of the street to look up at the skyscrapers, predict when and where they will stop and decide what move you will use to get around them.

The full, winding half-circle approach usually works when you see a clump of tourists, but you must begin walking in the semi-circle before you reach them. Then you will miss your opportunity to walk around them, and you will say "excuse me," and try to wade through them. There's a bunch right in front of me and I lose my racing opponent in the crowd for a minute in the crowd across the street, fearing he has turned a corner.

I pick him up, with my peripheral vision, and keep moving, twisting, and shouting, like Chubby Checker, as I go down the block.

At the end of the block, after I win the race… what the hell do I do now? Celebrate like I have won the Olympics? Hundreds of heads pass.

There is that feeling of a swinging pendulum again, inside. It's almost like I have no bottom or top to my thoughts now that

I have reached the end of the street. So, I just stop and stare in the black window of the store near a dead end. And there is a strange feeling inside, that nothing will ever fill me again, a strange kind of fear at everything that moves. It's like walking through the projects at four in the morning, when no one sits on the benches to assure you that normal life is going on. There is no destination or place that I'm going, and I am like a saxophonist in the middle of a solo who has lost his way.

I look in a coffee house window and the feeling does not leave me. The pastries look good, so I wander inside and follow the smell.

"Coffee cake and a large coffee."

"Got it."

I find a little corner and a television set. I lean against the wall and the hardness feels good. A beautiful girl with blue-green eyes brings me the coffee and cake.

The coffee feels good going down—something burning. The coffee cake is crumbly and satisfying, but the feeling deep down in my stomach that something is going to happen does not go away. I would call it impending doom, but it happens all the time. I can never chase away or minimize this feeling—I always concentrate on the smallest, dirtiest, most insignificant thing in the room and that thing symbolizes me. There's a small piece of dust at my feet near an opening at the base of the exposed brick wall. Mice could come through there and this is what I look at, not the throats of the beautiful girls waiting for theatres to open or the colorful dresses of the people speaking Creole, or the flowing gowns of the women walking up and down the block waiting for the Broadway shows or four-star restaurants to open. I am looking instead at a hole in the wall and thinking about the pain in my stomach. I could call it fear but it might be something else.

Right now, in the corner of this coffee shop, I'm as thin as a playing card. The congestion and beauty of a Manhattan afternoon awaits me outside, but I can't push the door open. The rush of people is too much, I am not feeling good; jostled and pressed in. The noise of the street ushers out some of this bad feeling and this bottomless pit returns. It is where I dwell, like a dude in those Edgar Alan Poe stories, removed from everything he sees.

Eventually, I get up and push at the door. The sunlight threatens to pry my blinking eyes open and the gorilla of doom returns. I feel like my stomach and everything around it is empty and will never be filled again. I find a ledge and sit. My knees start to shake a bit and my stomach feels like my stomach wants to be a part of another body. I find a step to sit on for a moment and it grips me—this time it starts in my stomach but comes over my back, a complete paralysis. I just sit there watching the pocketbooks and legs of women go past me. They are moving out of sync today—the legs follow the motion of the bags. I am frozen.

I head to the middle of the crowd. New York City is the easiest place in the world to get lost in, because everyone is intent on an imaginary or real destination. They ignore what is in front of their face. After all, it may be a Broadway illusion or the creation of a man with three hands playing a card game called Molly or a Julliard student playing violin in the subway, anything to stop the flat line of day to day. I hesitate for a moment, and everyone swirls around me, looking into the latest scheme. The dealer moves his hands so quickly, they seem invisible.

There are people in front of me and on the sides—I feel comforted but New Yorkers are masters at not touching people, so they move in front of me and around me and all I have to do is stand still. I pretend like I'm forgetting something and search in my pockets, looking down on the blonde and brown heads as they pass.

I stop again at the corner, following a student group, on a trip, with posters and the first time-in-the-big-city glow on their faces, making their pimples fade. They turn the corner quickly, and I immediately stare at the big kid, like me, leading up the rear, breathing deeply. Now, without high school basketball, most of my weight has moved to my chest and I'm sure I would look good in a military uniform.

A cave begins in the pit of my stomach. They are going to justify this war and they are going to send as many Black boys over there as they can. I have no rich father or student deferment or flat feet to protect me. I know nothing of this place they want to send me, Vietnam, but I am sure of one thing—America will never back down and that means putting the expendables in harm's way. I suppose White, lower-class dudes have the same problem—nothing to protect them legally while the government writes them one note that will make them a murderer and a liar at the same time. In America we have the right to determine our own governmental systems, shouldn't little yellow people have the same right? I don't know. Will the big nations always swallow up the little ones?

Even my throat is jumping, I find a vest pocket park bench in front of a man-made waterfall and just stare at the downpour. I stay, feeling the wind, watching the pressed pants crease in the men walking with expensive suits under London Fog raincoats. I will never be one of these men—all of this, the rush of Manhattan with a briefcase, going to a very important meeting, will never be me. I have no roadmap in a city where everyone comes with a plan or hatches one. Their devotion to task has killed mine. I wander in a strange land of tall buildings and leather briefcases.

There is nothing but the wall of Vietnam to hit my fucking head against. History is stopping and everybody is smashing, throwing the country against the consuming fire of this name—Vietnam—that none of us in South Jamaica ever heard before. Families throw rationales at each other like plates around the dinner table. The question is are you for or against this god damn war? What are we fighting for? And now, with this feeling of inevitability—someone else will be calling the shots the minute Walter Cronkite says so.

And it's one two three four/what are we fighting for?
Don't ask me /I don't give a damn/We're all going to Vietnam!

I get into the tempo and walk toward the library. Bryant Park is the place to sit, maybe cop a joint and enjoy the pace of others racing by to the library with the lions out front or down Fifth Avenue. Bryant Park seems like a concrete island of sanity in a city of people rushing thru life, becoming their own blur. I find the corner of a bench free and park my ass. It's not just the pace of the walking, but that look of urgency playing on the faces of New Yorkers.

Somebody's slow is somebody else's fast and I take out one

I rolled two days ago but never had the chance to smoke. 8.5 million, coming at you all coming at once.

Reefer slows me down, allows me to make my universe ease. *Richard against the world.* Pot makes me feel like I'm in a country glen in the middle of the horn honks, anxious legs and brows furrowed like an animal spying food.

New Yorker's legs become blurry and the slow pokes on the street look like they're moving at the same pace as the fast ones. My head feels like it might come off, but it's a good feeling and I lean back, as dawn creeps up like a robber. There is the New York City afternoon tired, shown in bags under the eyes--the afternoon is the time to wait, relax and pray for a second wind.

Maybe all of this will fit together somehow. Maybe I'll go over there and distinguish myself and come home to the waiting arms of Sandra. If only this were a fucking Disney movie but it ain't none of that—my buddies come back changed. Sandra has been known to step out a bit, but now I don't think she has since I've been messing with her. There's a dead ending to this back street—I must go to war and write letters home to her, and I can't see her from thousands of miles away in the dense ass jungle. So, there's nothing I can do, but have a few friends watch her, check her movements, or just give it the fuck up to God. That would be the mature way and Ma said there will be other women in my life—but I don't know that. Like the projects, Sandra feels and smells real to me and everything else is far away. I can touch Sandra with my hands, but ideas like governments are far away. So, Ma can talk about the new life on Union Hall Street, and I can imagine coming home to Sandra with Martha Reeves and the Vandellas singing in the background, but that's a movie yet to be made.

I might as well stroll down Broadway. The lights and motion

usually lift me up out of the gutter. The shiny cars and obedient chauffeurs are an exercise of imperialism and order. There is something reassuring about Broadway and Fifth Avenue—the *opulence*. People could be dying in the Bronx and there could be mass fires in Queens but the windows with manikins dancing the Tango, in the department store windows, will never be obliterated. The naked manikins will forever be in place.

I see the cars first and the lights; some are dingy, and some blown out but the bulbs from the marquees are reflected on the running boards. Furs, jewelry, and pretense; the nouveau riche never look down. I lean on a car for a moment watching the early entries to the theatre—sometimes you can catch actresses or actors scurrying in about an hour before curtain call.

The well-dressed tourists and the hicks from New Jersey pile in. The Jerseyites look down their noses at everyone and everything; they have cheap jewelry and suits that have been worn too many times. They hate what they do not understand. The women with real fortunes, stepping out of sleek black cars, with their luxurious legs and sequined gowns, own the street.

There is too much joy, so I head underground, to the subway, where parties are sometimes conducted in every car. The subway is party central. A boom box comes out, and the music is good, the subway car is transformed.

Even the White people bob their heads to the music and for a second, the city turns warm and there is an absence of fear of the pick pocket or murderer sitting right next to you. This subway car certainly is wild—with music going and dancing down at the end of the car. Teenagers run amuck. In the middle of the car, slick dressed dinner-goers chat as one homeless lady serenades us.

"This is the story of the homeless lady…"

It is a shorter walk home now. In the past few weeks, we have moved most of the boxes into the clumsy, dark house on Union Hall Street. My room is still cluttered and strange, but I manage to find the dirty journal.

Journal entry: February 1967
I want to be somebody someday, far away
from this place. I want to have a voice that
people can hear. Everybody's voice in South Jamaica
has been turned into a cough by too much
beer or reefer or heroin. Everyone rasps
and clings to the day with their fingernails
waiting to fall off. I want to soar and be
like the people on television—doing something
that will lift me from these walls and
the awful shaking inside. Once the shaking
stops, I'll be all right but there is so much sadness
down the dark alleys, men standing with
red eyes on the street corners, so much to
avoid. I want something to embrace.

I'm supposed to see Sandra before I leave, but I don't really want to. I mean, I do, and I don't. This is very close to goodbye and every time I touch her, it feels bittersweet.

It feels like I'm moving toward her and away from her at the same time. South Jamaica, with its sounds of Stevie Wonder, that blind boy with the harmonica in his mouth, and the spontaneous collections of people swinging on link chains in front of three-story brick buildings; the narratives in the morning of who fell to the needle last night—I will miss all of that, because it what I have been witness to, these nineteen years of my life.

And Sandra for me symbolizes this place that I love and do not love at the same time. Leaving is a terrible thing—and I will miss the voice of Miss Catherine, Sandra's mother, and the good advice she bellows at me.

I'll long for the basketball mornings, across the street from the projects, at five a.m. when I get out there before anyone else, feeling like the first man in the world. The concrete feels good and semi-cool beneath my Chuck Taylors. The sun has barely come up over the projects at five in the morning and I stop sometimes and watch the yellow sun creep over the buildings, like giving birth to a smile. And for a second, there are no narratives of my friends killing themselves with heroin, being alive one minute, and a ghost of dust, a missing character on a tragic stage the next.

Sandra says to come over Sunday night, when she's preparing for the week of school. This is when she lines up her shoes and her outfits, making choices from the plastic bags from the dry cleaner's. She is the best-dressed girl in the projects, wearing labels others cannot pronounce. Everything is dry cleaned and hung up in her closet. She seems ethereal and she is my escape from the cluster of the brown brick buildings I live in.

When I get there, she is ready, with incense and a long, flowing gown. Sandra is a statue tonight, like marble, and my hands slide off her. She seems distant and thinking about something else.

But when she returns from the bathroom and I put my hands under her gown, like I'm supposed to do, feeling her muscular thighs, I finger my way up to the silent place and she winces a little as I lay her down and my hand seems like it has eight fingers. Her skin feels foreign.

I press and move, thinking about the desolate hills of Vietnam, instead of her compendious breasts and I curl my body, making her forget about Sam Cooke singing:

I was born by the river...

I feel distance in my eyes as I think about the stomped-on grass and worn chain links of the projects. It will be a long time before I hear the girls and their rhymes with the jump ropes outside Sandra's window.

Mary Mack, Mack, Mack.
   All dressed in black, black, black...

My hands slip from her she lays there, with a quizzical frown on her face. She slides into the envelope of sleep, sure that I am leaving her and that this will be our last night together. The night is not silken; it is just dark.

I kiss her battered toes as I leave; her feet are about fifty years old, split bunions are forming from dancing. There's a bittersweet feeling in my stomach—a kind of dread moves to the tip of my fingers where I can smell her honey dew smell. The building seems asleep. I start down the street, after I make sure Catherine's front door is locked. Catherine is snoring, and the street seems to go on and on. The people behind the windows know I'm leaving home and the kids in the square continue to crack on one another as if the whole damn place is oblivious to this war for a brief second.

There are four guys standing in cashmere coats on the stoop and I don't know what they have in their pockets, so I turn quickly to the safety of Union Hall Street. Something is jumping within my chest.

CHAPTER THREE

I have the same jumpy feeling as we fly over the jungle; I hear the gunfire and see the smoke but the thing that scares me the most is the absence of human beings. All I can see are guns, bombs going off and then there is the bitter smell of Agent Orange.

I am number 256 in the battle to ram Democracy down the throats of little yellow people... Almost the moment I get off the chopper, I begin to think about scribblings things down on little pieces of paper; this is the way I will keep my mind together. Meaningless things, like a description of the red clay, the chocking air out in the front.

Air devoid of life; keeping the journal is sort of like talking to yourself and I keep up the conversation. When there is no one to talk to, there is always paper, and I can confide in my own vision, writing down what I see and not what the world is ramming in my ear.

This is the way I had to keep it together in South Jamaica—everyone telling me what I was, shouting at me from what their limited eyes and experience could see.

They send me somewhere near Khe Shan located in the Annamese Cordillera, the mountain range just to the east of the north-west corner of South Vietnam, officially assigned to the Ninth Cavalry Division.

In March 1968, an overland relief expedition (Operation Pegasus) was launched by a combined Marine–Army/ARVN task force that eventually broke through to the Marines at Khe Sanh. American commanders considered the defense of Khe Sanh a success, but shortly after the siege was lifted, the decision was made to dismantle the base rather than risk similar battles in the future. On 19 June 1968, the evacuation and destruction of KSCB began. Amid heavy shelling, the Marines attempted to salvage what they could before destroying what remained as they were evacuated. Minor attacks continued before the base was officially closed on 5 July. Marines remained around Hill 689, though, and fighting in the vicinity continued until 11 July until they were finally withdrawn, bringing the battle to a close.

In the aftermath, the North Vietnamese proclaimed a victory at Khe Sanh, while US forces claimed that they had withdrawn, as the base was no longer required. Historians have observed that the Battle of Khe Sanh may have distracted American and South Vietnamese attention from the buildup of Viet Cong (VC) forces in the south before the early 1968 Tet Offensive. Nevertheless, the US commander during the battle, General William Westmoreland, maintained that the true intention of Tet was to distract forces from Khe Sanh.

Our job is to fight with and support the Marines. They are trying to cut off and clear out a major roadway that leads to Khe Shan. Khe Shan is hilly and nasty with red clay, and we must dig and fight in bunkers with rats. There are leeches that seal into your skin and when you have time, you unscrew them, leaving a river of blood where the leech attached onto your leg and or arm, or head. When we are not fighting, in the rear, we pick them out of one another's skin, and we must sleep with towels on our heads.

President Johnson defended the importance of this battle by positing that thousands of Vietcong were coming in from Loas, through Khe Shan to join up with their Vietcong brothers.

This passageway from Laos to Vietnam had to be cut off. Ho Chi Min stirred the pride and history many Vietnamese by being able to fight off the French and others trying to lay claim to this strategic strip of land. He called the Americans invaders and threats to Vietnam's self-determination. We were the last line of defense to shut down this passageway and influx of the enemy. The constant rain and mist make it hard to catch a breath.

This is one the longest battles of the war and the Marines report that the Viet Cong sealed in some six thousand Marines, Army support and South Vietnamese Rangers. Many thought that the battle at Khe Shan could be exactly like the battle at Dien Bien Phu—which was a fucking a massacre for the French.

This was the sign from God that the French could not fight guerila warfare. The Vietcong presented a new style of ferocious fighter the French had never seen, and they saw the French as invaders. Ho Chi Min capitalized on the hatred for the American invaders and his movement LMF, eventually became the vicious Vietcong in our view. For the Vietnamese, he was a liberator. We had been propping the French up with money and military aid for years, then they handed the football to us.

Even though we had been supplying the French with weapons, we were not sending troops there. But America took the handoff of war and started to send "military advisors" and to "train" the South Vietnamese. This football was handed from president to president. LBJ was sold on the idea of growing Russian influence, and he made speeches about Communist invaders as John Kennedy had done, once his philosophic commitment was there, so were seventy-five thousand or more boys on the ground in the jungle.

The battle of Khe Shan was very important to the US military. According to the White House, the road was being used to let the communist forces in Vietnam. They were being trained in Laos and then Ho Chi Min would let his forces go. On January 29th, 1968, there were four divisions of Vietcong in the area of Khe Shan ready to strike; General Eastmoreland estimated 4,000 Vietcong in the area.

There were strategic hills, the 861 complex, the 861 A Hill complex. The artillery and air supports were monumental; the Americans were poised to use 81millimeter motors and M-79 Machine guns.

Some compared this battle to the battle at Dien Bien Pho, in importance.

They Vietcong hoped this would do the same thing to America as Ho Chi Min and his boys had done to the French. The VC had a formation planned to swarm the American forces by attacking them from the outside. The Americans used 4.2 mortars and Howitzers. The Americans are well supplied; for approximately three months the boys were working—building platforms and a landing strip for B-52's. Mail, rations, weapons had been dropped from the sky. On February 13th there was an attack, just 400 miles outside the perimeter. General Eastmoreland told his troops to stop advancing and to "button up." The ground troops were halted, while the B-52's dropped 500–750-pound bombs on the Vietcong. On March 25th the enemy closed in, after a tense wait, when soldiers cooked, and smoked and waiting. On 26 March, 1968, the enemy closed in.

The Communists are surprised by the preparedness of the Marines, Navy, Air Force and Army. On March 27th due to the barrage of bombing from the b-52's one and a half Vietcong units withdrew, and the enemy retreated, leaving Highway 9, a conduit from Laos to Vietnam in American control.

The scorched earth left behind looked like a movie set. Everything had been burned and scared by napalm. It looks like the world is truly coming to an end.

I find myself alone my hole at night and I begin another journal; I like being alone, but this is different over here. Over here, I feel I might never talk to or touch another human being, like I'm on the edge of the world about to fall off. The nights here are too deep; I feel like I can't touch anyone, like the darkness takes away my ability to stretch out and find another human being. Air is death, the cadavers that have been left behind to create a deep body owning chilling smell that shakes your core and causes pains in your chest dragging you under the earth with them.

    We are expecting an attack in days.

It comes earlier and we are pinned in our bunkers, groveling with the rats, trying to avoid enemy fire, again. Bombs blast and there is nothing we can do. There is the sound of fire from our artillery and we reach a landing, but then some our M-16s jam, after three rounds, and must be reloaded. I saw one, two men dead. Sometimes clusters of dead, they were waiting for us to return to camp. Bobby traps abound and mines; the Vietcong swing from trees, and we fight with M-16s, knives and bombs, fists in the futile air. The key is not to move or even light a match. A lit match could mean instant death.

The enemy will see us, and all our memories of a first kiss or prom are gone. And the pictures of our mothers in the center of our foreheads will suddenly age. Our father's voices are far off, and we stumble toward a light, in our near distance. All around. Pieces of bodies, guns shoes, bullets through the head. Groups of dead.

I lose it, and there is nothing but bombs going off in my head. I have my M-16 and I continue to fire into the flashing gun air. The lights and bombs flash and I fire three rounds, my M-16 jams again, amid the fire, watching forms fall in the darkness, illuminated only by bomb light.

I shoot and yell, at the same time, retching my guts up, until something snaps within my mind, the lights are too close to my eyes as my buddies scream out, I dodge the bullets, feeling something cool on my legs, like piss but it is blood, and I whirl like a child on merry-go-round, into the mud, with blood spurting out of my legs and arms. I try to put pressure on the wounds, then my head starts spinning, and the shooting speeds up as my vision blurs. I hear the fire as I crawl among the rats and leeches, making the ditch redder than Georgia clay with blood. I have one grenade left. I lift it detonate and throw into the air. It is my last-ditch effort to save my life. It may hit American soldiers, or it may cause enemy death. I have nothing left inside but a shred of spirit. One, two, lights cover me, and I am blinded again. The night blows apart, I sink to the bottom of the pothole with blood smeared all over me, hoping the rats do not devour me, as the grenade creates a flash of fire and power that knocks me down.

I don't know when or why the sun came up, but it did. I could hear Wee Willie's voice, at least he is alive. Those of us that can help carry stretchers with brothers on it to the platform where the copters are, do so. The helicopters and medical personal are all over while the fire never ceases in the air and bombs explode. Nothing stops the medical personal or Medevac; they will come in later. They are heroes like those laying near me. Those that will never sleep nestled in the arms of any woman.

The smell of death is all over my body. Gases fill the air, with the smoke and aftermath of new fire. I choke because the smell is not around me, it is within me and seeing the bodies strewn about, walking around dead brothers and headless bodies, snaps me into action. I instantly start carrying wounded soldiers on the stretchers to the helicopters that are all around, just by instinct—I have no energy.

The copters with medical personnel arrive quickly when the skies are black with bombs and fire smoke. I choke back my spittle and pick up another fallen brother, my breath is almost cut off with the deep bass smell of carnage. And I sink into the earth, trying to still hold on to the stretcher of a dead brother.

Two weeks later, we are still living in the trenches with the rats, but we have set up a few tents and we have what could be called the remnants of a base and a reinforced perimeter.

Wee Willie catches me writing in my tent; and tells the whole fucking unit that I'm the heir apparent to Ernest Gaines. Hardly. Sometimes, I write letters home for the illiterate and those that have problems saying what they mean. For a price, I create dreams.

I sometimes fail, but the writing is always better than theirs would have been.

Now, I'm writing a letter for a brother, a fellow soldier. I told him about my story with Sandra and he hired me to write a letter to his "left behind". We call the girls back home "left-behinds."

Now that sounds negative, but we really don't feel that way—but there's nothing else to call them. That life seems like a former life, something we can only imagine now. With cadaver smells comingling in the air, and bodies everywhere, there is the thought that the old life will disappear.

I've been here a month, and just like prison, you must join a group—in prison it might be skinheads or the Muslims but in the 'Nam there are two dominant groups—Blacks and Whites, just like home.

Unfortunately, the Nam gives birth to a group of cliques. The groups are based on whether you are for or against the war, but when we leave the back and go to the front, to battle every fighting man is the same.

If we numb ourselves, with pot, then none of this exists, for the duration of the high. But the minute we go out, the smell of cadavers is turning our stomachs, hard to get used to the flying awareness of death, riding the lightning bolts of fire called napalm. Forcing itself down our nostrils, making our chests pain. Marijuana takes some of the sting out of war temporarily.

The "villes" or villages are the small streets and almost towns, where we never fight or bomb. There is a semblance of real life in the "villes."

Vietnamese children are going back and forth to school.

In the "back" where we are, the battle for Vietnam seems far away, the America civil war is still being fought as people party in racial and cultural groups, with southerners and northerners on different sides. In the front we are all one. It's that simple—some of us believe all the propaganda and shit, that the United States government is pitching, about winning the war and others think that everything they say is a lie.

The White boys believe in the dream. They think they have something to defend—and that's all right.

Somehow, Black people from home are placed in the same unit. Some said it was done by social security number and that there is a beginning number that only Black men have.

Zero. An unknown entity.

Wee Willie had been here for a few months when I got here, and Jimmy Boudwin and Charlie Leslie were already in fatigues. Majour thinks they choose us by social security numbers. Headley is here too. They all from the South Jamaica, Queens area.

Wee Willie, my ace boon coon in the projects, is always in a good mood, even in war. There seems to be a party going on in his head.

There are two distinct camps—the Blacks and the Whites, but there are splinter groups—Chicanos are higher ups, Latinas are usually officers, and every cultural group you can name, except the African American soldiers are the grunts. Like back home, people of color's heads are on a swivel, looking for the next attack. I only received one official letter from the American government in my life and it was the draft notice. The Latinos sort of keep to themselves but the civil war is fought daily in whispers and looks and gestures.

Wee Willie stands too close to them, almost like he enjoys their acceptance. I want him to stand away from the bunches of

Whites and just look at them, seeing their snide smiles, hearing the jokes they make about his dark skin when he is not listening. They think he is their minstrel, but Wee Willie is too smart for them, I just know it. He laughs and jokes with them and I never do. I stand back from them, keeping away from the Whites in the unit when we are not fighting.

When we are not in the front, everyone is segregated, but when we are fighting, we are one. Wee Willie is a little gullible. He will believe what the White man says. I know White people are lying because their mouths are moving.

Wee Willie is talking shit. He is up early today. He seems like his old self but I'm leery; he looks like the people from *Invasion of the Body Snatchers* after their souls have been gutted. Bubba Cee is up early also, eating rations and looking strange.

"Wee Willie, what are you doing, man?"

Bubba Cee thinks the Black soldiers are here for his entertainment. It's early morning and he wants to watch television.

"I heard you could dance, Wee Willie," Bubba Cee says.

"I hear your mother could dance."

"I heard you could do the James Brown and the Ike Turner."

"What the hell are you talking about, White boy?"

"You know your people know how to cut a rug..."

"I got your people, bitch," I say.

"There you go again. Mr. Black Panther over there, getting a little too sensitive."

"Mr. Black Panther, huh? Why you always making fun of things you don't understand?"

"Oh, why don't I understand it?"

"Maybe it's because you never read a book on the Black

Panthers or ever tried to understand the needs of an oppressed people."

"You sound like a textbook; just talk to me."

"I am talking to you; you just don't understand what it's like to come from the rough side. You ever read Franz Fanon?"

Shapiro is all right. I just hope they don't do in Shapiro. He's much too progressive for the others.

"Stop all the talking, ladies, and get ready to move your pretty asses out," shouts Lieutenant Wrong. He will march us into danger if he thinks there's a medal in it for him. Once, he has the co-ordinates, he stops thinking, and he leads the grunts into danger, thinking only about his personal glory. Some Lieutenants do not lead; they ignore warnings that come over the radio and seek medals for themselves, not all of them but many.

The air is especially choking today. I can't even cough as I "march" over the intimidating clay. The awful red clay, roads are dusty and acrid when they're not saturated with water and endless rain. I hate walking because it makes your boots feel even heavier and stirs the dust up from the awful earth.

Rations taste like home-made shit, to me. Some of the guys really like the food, they add beef and some of the dishes are pretty good.

The purpose of smoking and staying up all night, is to get as high as hell and forget that you are in a war. To numb yourself to all that is and everything you will have to confront when you return to battle. If we can drown out the sound of bombs and fire with good drugs, then so be it.

I am used to momma's cooking, and I miss the aromas rising from her pots and pans; the rain is continuous. The arresting smell of brothers left behind makes it difficult to inhale. Inhaling deeply causes pain. I flinch. I wince and wheeze with the others, but no one pays our small concerns any attention. After all, we are soldiers and our task is our mission, and the completion of the mission is the only thing that matters.

I never believed any of that dedication to country shit, but late at night when it is cold here, you want to trust in something. Most days, I spend moving away from feeling but there is wind and the memory of home. I used to fucking feel things, but now I try not to let anything penetrate my surface; the goal is to wall everything out and to try and get some sleep but I turn over and over seeing the faces on the bench, hearing the voices of the projects in my head, waiting for the enemy to arrive, when I think I have already seen him in the mirror.

CHAPTER FOUR

I'm at war inside myself. If I believe like the White boys believe, then it could be easier to dehumanize the yellow people. It is easy to dehumanize those that look, act, and pray differently than you.

But I know that the true liars in my life have had red skin and not yellow. When the Vietnamese say, "not your war," it means that they know we do not have planes or runways or bombs, and they know who is burning off their skin. The Black soldiers are caught in a vice, and it is crushing our heads, making thoughts maze-like and confused. Who do you believe? If the night raids are correct, then enemies are not human beings, just objects to be obliterated. But I have never been on a night raid—killing innocent, thin-limbed people like they used to kill captured Africans, throwing us overboard, like too much cargo.

To go out with the Whites, to harm the innocent, you must convince yourself that the enemy doesn't matter. It's a killer mindset, but you must remind yourself that you're still a human fucking being. Some Vietcong children and women lure Americans into traps or kill them with razors and knives. It is hard to know who an enemy combatant is.

There are some tender moments.

I keep writing the letters home for the unit guys, for a price. As I get better and better with the prose, the prices rise.

In two days, we are to leave the back and move to the front with the expressed purpose of destroying access on the road that leads to Laos. Little is explained to us by the brass; we must be ready to move at a moment's notice. Like back home, someone else is calling the shots and we are pawns being moved by larger fingers.

Lieutenant Wrong, with his technical equipment and assistants, is always the last to know our unit's future coordinates and he does not think about the surrounding dangers in the jungle. The Vietcong are always watching us, and they appear to have formations and movement choreographed and we seem to be just feeling out way with the help of two people: the radio man and his boy. But everything, the final action is decided by Lieutenant Wrong, whether to move or stay put or march into an ambush. He is the director, and we are his reluctant grunts.

There's always desperation in Lieutenant Wrong's eyes; he looks like a caged dog. He's five-five with a slight build. The Lieutenant and his radio man ain't fooling nobody. He is totally dependent on that little black box—they shout coordinates and questions about where the yellow people might be, but there is never any certainty.

The Viet Cong ain't where the brass thinks they will be because this is a different kind of warfare. This is not conventional, fought in the jungle—our officers don't know a damn thing about the enemy and their habits. Those little suckers are smarter than we are, and this is their backwoods. They usually put three or four brothers in the lead, hoping we will get shot and then America will dispose of the bodies later. Today, they put Headley, Charlie Leslie, and Wee Willie in the front of the line. Headley is so stupid and boastful that he thinks it's a promotion to be at the point. That is the most dangerous place to be, at the head of the line. Headley is a good example of a guy who is trying his best to cover up fear with bravado. It's easy to spot that kind—chest sticking out but really his tail is firmly planted between his legs. You can't cover up fear; it just gets larger and more visible. Wee Willie is third in line, crouching behind Charlie Leslie.

The bullets are whizzing, and the sound and cadence of the firing creates a kind of strange rhythm that brings comfort to my ears; the firing is incessant, sealing within my brain. We never see the enemy—we just fire into smoke, taste smoke, watching the fire darts of napalm.

The air has a tinge of red for some reason and I feel a nagging pain in my back and a sharp bolt in my kidneys, and a metallic smell at the back of my throat; something they say I just must get used to.

CHAPTER FIVE

The shiny Cadillac of Democracy is now discarded. Some of us are starting to question what we hear—we all thought it was a war to save Democracy, but it seems to be a battle for a little strip of land that everybody wants. The domino theory might be correct but there are signs that Laos will not go the way of Ho Chi Min. We are dumping tons of bombs on Laos. Everyone in Washington is in the full-time business of convincing the nation that communism will come into your living room if it succeeds in Vietnam. That's a long commute, buddy.

It is November, 1968, and LBJ is talking "peacekeeping officers" and withdrawal, while more boys come. It seems every few months or so he comes up with new propaganda, testing the waters and the American appetite for losing more boys and girls. It is a shame because this war was handed to LBJ, and he tries to carry the awful load. Even though America is reluctant to admit it, we all knew the "military advisors" were something more. Kennedy could have stopped with advisors. They were really ground troops.

The rationales for the aggression and escalation of the war, the coated words, and falsehoods seem to age President Johnson. His hound dog face is becoming more jowly and blood vessels are bursting in his eyes. My mother saves front page of the *New York Times* and when we have mail call—two times a month I have enough letters to read for weeks and fourteen front pages from the paper of record. I stack my letters and read each front page of the *New York Times* according to date. The American people seem to want to withdraw from Vietnam. They are tired of losing their sons and daughters to a nebulous vision.

"MAIL! MAIL!"

We are in the back for a while. That is where the partying and smoking takes place.

We just got some new herbs, so we gather in segregated groups, to get high as hell, and tell lies about women we haven't been with after the perimeter has been secured, guarded and we feel the safety of the back.

We are in a circle, smoking the shit out of some pot, trying to forget that we will have to return to-- the flashing fire and incessant bombs of the front.

Flashlight, instant death. Light a cigarette instant death. Any movement that gives away position means that a young boy before he smiles at the birth of his own child or know the verisimilitude of a woman, he has been cut down, like a flower leaving only the stalk. We know what waits for us out where the battle rages and we do not want to see it, just for a moment, and pretend we are not in a war. That's why we get blind on herbs and try to fill the air with something other than the lingering smell of last breaths.

We will soon be marching again and that means lost life for us or someone close to us. The most important moments involve anything from home.

Bobby is hopeful that he'll get a letter of commitment from his girl. I can't promise results; all I can do is write the fucking letter. He has those strange eyes—with too much white in them. His eyes don't stare, they just stay open. There is something missing in his stare, almost as if someone has pulled out his skull a long time ago and he is speaking through the worms coming from his eyes.

I remember his was syrupy...

Susan,

When you get this, I might be dead in the rice paddies, but our love will extend far beyond the time you get the final news. Nothing will make me forget our last lovemaking. It gets a little distant with time, but I can still feel your hands running across my body. The last time we made love stays with me. I think about your shaved legs in the middle of this nasty place, and I reach out in the humid air and pretend I'm touching you. You are so foreign to anything here—everything in the 'Nam is gruff. We have one job here. We must kill more of them than they do of us. Every man is just a number sent forth to make McNamara and Johnson happy... with escalation.

Most of the letters are not that graphic but when they want to remind the girl of the last time, they were together, it gets visual. They try to recreate the world they've left, but there is nothing to reach and feel here. What they don't realize is that they can't do a damn thing to change the course of fate. They are thousands of miles away in a wet jungle and Jody lives right next door.

Jody got your girl and gone... that was the lyric of the day.

He might be some young guy that they had their eye on for a few years and now he's of age or some old bastard that's been waiting, but he is there, and you are in Vietnam. Everybody is frustrated over what they can't control—their women at home, the finances, and the kids—while they are marching in mush, the universe is slowly falling apart back home and there ain't a damn thing they can do about it. Either way, soldiers are helpless, and this makes them feel more resentment—they're already mad as hell because they must be over here.

MY DEAREST SUSAN,

Late at night, I console myself by knowing that you are still mine. When I'm coughing and inhaling dust, I think of your skin. When I can only touch dirt, I think of your silken touch. I am surrounded by gunfire, and I want to touch the edges of your fingers and for one-half of a microsecond, then I will feel alive. I'd like to be more positive, but the moment is dashed with the demanding voice of my Lieutenant. The day is broken, and I must march through the red clay.

LOVE,
Bobby

Lieutenant Wrong calls, "Come on, ladies…"

The war drains me and hangs around like another body.

In 'Nam, Wee Willie needed a girl dancing in front of him, something reminiscent from home, but each day made us aware of the futility of his wish. There is nothing that resembles home—whenever we find a semblance, we latch onto it. William is the quintessential American—he believed in the Ozzie and Harriet world and the promises of television. There should be a mom and dad and two children—but that was not the life we saw in war. All the Ozzie and Harriet dreams were obliterated.

He is sometimes depressed because Vietnam is like bands of hell wrapped around each other, compared to home. Each band had its own character and name.

Wee-Willie had memorized the script of most of the shows, and for fun he would recite the characters' lines and I would imagine I had a small black-and-white television set. It's a game we play at night, while smoking and partying when we are in the back--television reminds us of home. I am the sound effects man, and he becomes the voices of the characters, until the entire game is senseless and makes everyone realize how far they are away from normal television, hot dogs, and big breasted girls running on the beach. All of us wonder if we will return to those subtle Americanisms.

None of us can reconcile what we see with what we have heard. The words of propaganda and dedication are lost because it looks as if we are forcing our will on people who do not want us here.

All the Vietnamese look with gaseous eyes that only threaten. This is all hard for Wee Willie to take—he likes acceptance. At home, he liked people, and they adored his flash and smile. Now, over here, there is no family and no crowd on the park bench to entertain. His brother, Anthony, writes him to let him know that his mother needs to have her leg amputated due to diabetes. Anthony is hopelessly strung out and it seems like things haven't changed in the niggerhood. After a few months, Wee Willie starts to mope around the base. I pull him to the side in the dirt to talk.

"When did you start feeling so fucking depressed?"

"Months ago. It was like carrying a fucking weight around. It's so hard to explain, I can't tell you. It takes me over in a second. I'd start thinking about back home or family and then I'd look to the hills and see smoke and the return of fire. Then you came and shit seemed possible again; you reminded me of the old niggerhood.

"And now?"

"If I see one more fire or another sky full of black smoke, I might turn the M16 on myself," he says, with his eyes getting wide, backing up a bit.

"Ain't no suicide hotline out here, no one-eight-hundred numbers, Jack. You got to do it for yourself. Maybe you need to talk to a Chaplin?"

"This ain't no religious dilemma. I've just seen too much. You remember, when we were growing up, somebody would overdose every damn day. There's just so much a human being can take. I've seen too much dying. What does the world expect from me?"

"Yeah, yeah, you're just full. It's like a glass, man, or a Coke that's been all shook up. You just need to calm down, let the carbonated air out a little bit, man. That's all."

"We don't have much, do we? I mean home was hell and now here in the fucking jungle. What has life been for us?"

"A world of hurt man. My mother used to say you're born with two strikes against you. Your Black and you're a man, jail is the third strike. Just concentrate on putting one foot in front of the other. Don't dwell on the fucking past—think about the footprint you're about to make."

"Got it. But what do I do with the feelings? I think I might have that post traumatic shit or something, bra, but I can't stuff the feelings down anymore. I must fucking do something, man. There's a party in my head and I'm not invited. There is too much going on. Just too much fucking going on."

"Look, man, why don't you come in the tent, get a Coke."

"Fuck a fucking Coke, man. Fuck a Coke. I need something

more than a damn drink. I need somebody to talk to me, man. Why is it that one race of people gets all the fucking pain?"

"I know, man, just come on in and talk to me for a minute."

"Damn that shit homes. I got to do something."

Willie searches in his pants like he's looking for something. His face is full of veins. Willie takes out a revolver and points it to his head.

"Wee Willie. No. Man—noooo!"

"I'm sick of this shit, man. I'm sick of this shit."

He breaks down into tears. I go over and wrap my arms around his shoulders and finger the cold steel of the gun. I reach around him and plan my strategy.

"No, man. No." I hold him, and he starts sobbing. He literally shakes like a fucking leaf in my arms.

"This ain't the way, man. Turning all that shit in on yourself. This ain't the fucking way. Come on, man. Come with me. Like the old days—you knew what I was about to do before I did it, like brothers."

"But this ain't no basketball game, man. This is 'Nam."

I put him in a half nelson, trying to take the gun away from him. His muscles flex as we wrestle to the jungle floor. I reach over him, using my height, as he bucks with back muscles. I manage to finger the gun away from his ass. The revolver feels alien as he moves his fingers away from the trigger. I hug his shoulders like I used to do at half-time in a tough basketball game. After minutes, he stops shaking. I throw the revolver over into the dirt.

I kept Willie from killing himself tonight but who will stop me?

CHAPTER SIX
TET OFFENSIVE

All we knew was that there would be a barrage of bombs and the air would look like a bad World War II movie and we could expect to be pinned down and surrounded.

I take refuge in the repetition of my M-16 that only allows me to shoot a few rounds and then it jams, and I must clean it and reload, the weapon hits hard against my stomach muscles. I am always hungry for home, and it might not just be home cooking, but the feel of the gun is good.

I stand amid dust and flying shit; the smell of Agent Orange and chemicals float in air. I can taste something metallic at the back of my tongue. Napalm's fire is in my mind. I feel the nakedness of my gun when I hold it close to me, seeking some sort of peace but there is none and I want to run up a hill somewhere. I can barely hear the barking voices over the radio. All the marching orders and useless words float in air. I continue to shoot at an enemy that I cannot see.

"Richard... Cover!"

I see some broken concrete in the distance; this must be the fucking town they were talking about.

I break out and start to fire just over the Lieutenant's head. The enlisted men try to protect him. The front of the line is still moving. This is a broken place, where civilization used to be. Return of fire and the first five boys are engaged. I run behind a tree for cover and keep firing while others scurry for walls.

Bullets box my ears.

"Richard, where the fuck are you?"

"Firing, sir."

My shoulder feels like lead. Hours of fire and return. The rays of dark sunlight stream through. Lieutenant Wrong orders us to the center of what was once a street with businesses and families, from what the men in the unit are saying. I follow, feeling like sheep. My gut wants to let go but I hold my vomit. Lieutenant Wrong peels back a little and spies me; I'm tired but still firing. There are baby tombstones in his eyes. We just fire back against the flashes from enemy guns.

"I don't know exactly where we are. We need bombs. Planes. I have fucking men dying. It all looks the fucking same out here. I have no idea where the heck we are. One marsh looks like the next. One hill looks like the next."

The Viet Cong know the terrain—this is their jungle and country, and we are feeling our way. The enemy's strategy was to pull us in the center and then attack from all sides. We walked into the ambush.

There is no reprieve; over a hill, in the next clearing, between the stalks of these horrible jungle bushes, there is still fire.

"Help us, reinforce us. Fucking help, us," he shouts as if his voice is fading. After what seems like hours, reinforcements come as the blades begin to darken and cut the sky in a thousand pieces as American bombs own the air.

In the back, away from the fighting, home is all we talk about. The hope is to take care of everything in the back of you and everything in front. I have letters stacked, about twenty I have not read.

I ache for 109th Ave.; I miss it like a hand permanently out of the protection of a glove.

I can only imagine the brown bar of my mother's arm and the worth I would feel in her caress but that feels like it is long gone.

Like most soldiers, I'm trying to keep it all together. I want to believe that things are fine at home but sometimes I think I'm fooling myself.

MOMMA,

Diabetes is not a death sentence. People are living with the condition and changing their lives with diet and exercise. You're used to jumping in the car when you want to go someplace. Think of taking a bus or walking where you want to go. If you walk a block or two one day, walk three the next and then four…

You might get together with some other ladies that are walking the shopping centers to lose weight. All of us in the family have to stop eating fried foods and bacon and eggs.

You know, I know a little about a battle of life and death; that's what this is. You must fight for your life just like you're telling me. Take care of yourself. We've come over a lot of obstacles, moving to the north from the south and we never let what they're doing stop us. Now that we're here, we have to fight for our existence every day. Above all, to "thine own self be true". If something happens to you, we all will lose our devoted mother, so please try to stay away from that "slavery food". I am fine, no injuries, and holding up well. If I get the smallest injury, I'll fill you in on all the details. I won't hold nothing back.

The key though, with eating, is to develop good habits and replace what you used to do with something different. And you know most of the older members of our family—and some of the younger ones—have a love affair with that bottle. Alcohol can only take you down and it's not to be mixed with your diabetes medication, so please be careful. I want to make sure I have you and a home to return to.

It all comes down to eating the wrong stuff: the slavery food—anything from a pig, anything that just gives you fats and carbohydrates—that is the wrong stuff.

Love,
Richard

She writes back with shaking letters.

Son

All I can say is that I did not raise you for this. I took you to church every Sunday and made your education the priority, but you ended up here, in this terrible war. I wanted you to be a man of peace and maybe study for the ministry. America has her needs though and those are more important than the concerns of one mother, I guess. They never wrote you before; they waited until you were eighteen to write you and that was an invitation to over there. So, all of that is balled up inside of me—you were thinking about college while you were here. You have a good mind if it's put to something constructive, something other than killing people. Don't let the service change you; it changed Harish, Amos, and James. They all came back with a basement look in their eyes that made their bodies shrivel up. They crawled in the bottle, and it broke. I just know that you will come out the other side of this stronger, because I know my son. I raised you to be better than the people around you—if you remember, I told you that you were better than the dope fiends and the drug dealers around here, and you probably have some of those people over there too. You are better than anyone that would lead you into perdition. Don't follow the Devil; he is plain to see, and you can trace his tracks. His form is easy to recognize.

I appreciate your words, but I must eat what I have to eat because of my nerves. I think about you and your brother all the time and I can call that fool but I can't reach you and you ~~were~~ are my pretty little brown child. I can never forget your smile and I know I will see you again soon.

Son, I tried some of the things you told me but the food tastes better fried. I have just been eating that way all my life. It's hard to change old habits. I'm starting to feel a little bit better but every day I worry about you. I can't get through my day without wondering if you're doing well... self-preservation is the first law of nature, like you reminded me. Do just enough to get by and then look for an exit, some way of living until the next day.

You must live one minute, hour, second at a time and remember "this too shall pass". Don't worry about home; I can take care of all that. Concentrate on survival. Think about what Harriet Tubman and our ancestors had to live through—the lash and the hanging tree. Remind yourself of their dark days and struggle to see a streak of light between the bullets...

So, take heart and keep your head down.
Ma

When the letters are sparse, desperation takes hold, and some feel home has disappeared. There are two mail calls per month, and everyone expects at least two weeks of mail, so that they can read the letters slowly, enjoy them.

Many of the guys have been talking about suicide and some days it sounds like a real option, especially when you haven't heard from home in a while. I know that sounds crazy but it's true; the notion of the ending of a life, your own life, can make you feel better—at least then the pain and marching with soaking boots, piss, and shit in holes in the earth, will be over. It exerts some power over a totally chaotic situation. This is not the world but after a few months it sure seems to be. There is something beyond the trees and the bombs, but life seems squashed here, DE bowled.

Every day drags like a body. Some count the days, but I would rather crawl into the asshole of these dismal hours, seeing each minute, experiencing this death with my chest out, looking at it as if it is a horror movie I am experiencing again and again.

I always have suicide as a friend—I can run into the fucking bushes and blow my own head off and end the sound of whistling bombs, stomach wrenching cadaver smells, and stop seeing the flashing gun fire, sharing my bunker with rats or hearing the constant argument over the boomerang of history.

Bubba Cee and his boy, the Professor, are talking again. The Professor disengages and makes a beeline toward me. Shapiro runs away from them like he's seen a ghost.

"I know you don't want a letter. You can write your own. You're eloquent as they come, Professor," Richard says.

"But it's better if someone else writes it. Raid tonight. You in?"

"Are you in? Have they talked you into this crazy shit,

Professor?"

"Tonight, might be the first. Nihilism man. None of this war or anything we do here matters," he said turning his palms up to the bomb filled sky.

"Bullshit. It all matters. The minute we give in to it, we're lost."

"I hear you, but my mind keeps telling me fuck it. Fuck it. Go."

"I hate to hear that, Professor. I thought you were against humanity acting in fucked up ways."

"I was but last night I heard a baby crying and it was a strange curdling cry like I had never heard in my life. It sounded like the baby had seen something she would never forget. Like she was crying for all of humanity, man. For all of us and everything we've seen. My damn skin crawled and something let go inside. I don't know what it was—it was like a damn burst, or a wall being hammered by concrete and finally falling apart."

"Build the wall again."

"You've been a pretty good friend. I hope I can stand with you but there's pressure."

"What do you mean? From Bubba Cee?"

"From all of them. I feel more comfortable with you and Majour. You guys think. You're different than the rest."

Professor turns and waddles back, as if he is ashamed of himself. He looks like an impudent child. Shapiro stares at me with eyes of stone. He sees through some of this, but I question his ability to repel the stupidity of the others. He seems like someone extracted his guts a long time ago, but his heart and his head are still working.

CHAPTER SEVEN

Insomnia. When I try to sleep, I hear movement. Feet. I roll over and search for stars through the jungle. I can see nothing in front of me and I'm afraid that if I sleep, I will awake to gun flashes and bugs crawling over cadavers. Leeches lodge in my head and I unconsciously turn them and screw them out, leaving a circle of blood. The rats scurry in the bunker and have family meetings.

For one brief second, as I look over the hill, I can see nothing but a man talking to a buffalo. This must have been a serene place once. I never bother even looking for the moon.

There are so many deaths that occur, and I feel less and less attached to anything but the cold steel of my M-16. The letters from home make me feel some connection, but I am out here, alone, especially when I am on patrol. It's almost like there's a metal plate hiding my feelings. If you get too attached to the man next to you, he may be gone the next day and then what do you have left? There is no sound for a moment and I am on the rim of sleep. I'm in that way station where my eyes are closed but I can sense and hear everything around me. I'm often in this state—not fully asleep and not awake. Occasionally, I open my eyes to check to see if what I'm hearing is real.

Yells. Women with searing voices own the air as they are assaulted. Children scream gut-wrenching screams. So close. I grovel for a second, but the bullets are not directed toward Black but yellow skin. The screams never stop, the voices drill holes in my head.

The leadership knows about this. The Bubba Cee crowd comes back with triumphant limbs, bloody fingers in their pockets and severed ears pasted to their helmets. I'm awake now. I fight the urge to throw up; I hold onto my rations for spite. The next morning Bubba Cee's eyes are clear with retribution.

"Yo, Richard. How'd you sleep?"

"Not well. Kept hearing cries during the night."

"That damned 'Nam. That's what you brothers call it, right?"

"Yeah. What's your point?"

"My point is that you guys got your own lingo, your own little society, right?"

"You got a purpose standing here?"

"Yeah, I still want you to write my letter, man."

"I can't. I have to believe in what I'm writing."

"What are you? Some kind of fucking monk, man? This is the 'Nam. Let go of that holier-than-thou shit for a moment, huh! Be like the fucking rest of us."

"This is me, man. I'm not your image of a Black man."

"And never the twain shall meet?"

"You said it."

"Fuck you two times, Richard."

"You wish you could, bitch. Then I could get off my hand."

CHAPTER EIGHT

"Charlie Company llth Division suspected of My Lai Massacre"

Early morning on March 16, 1968, helicopters carrying U.S. soldiers flew into a tiny village on the eastern side of South Vietnam, bordering the South China Sea. They'd arrived by a series of hamlets, known as My Lai, expecting to find a booby-trapped stronghold of their enemy, the Viet Cong. Instead, all they saw were noncombatants: women, children, elderly men. Many of them were preparing for breakfast.

The Americans, with about hundred soldiers from the American Army's division, a separate division, proceeded to massacre them. Over the next several hours, the civilians in My Lai (pronounced "Me Lie") and an adjacent settlement were shot and thrown in ditches. The body count: five hundred and four people from more than two hundred and forty families. Some women were raped. Huts and homes were burned. Even the livestock was destroyed.

It was one of the worst American military crimes in history and still pierces the collective conscience of Vietnam War veterans. On Friday, an organization called the Vietnam Peace Commemoration Committee is scheduled to hold a vigil in Lafayette Square across from the White House to acknowledge the American war crimes at My Lai.

Right after the attack, the soldiers—who had been told by

their superiors the night before that everyone they'd see would be a Viet Cong guerrilla or sympathizer—kept quiet about what they'd done.

The Mỹ Lai massacre was the **mass murder of unarmed South Vietnamese civilians by United States troops** in Sơn Tịnh District, South Vietnam, on 16 March 1968 during the Vietnam War. Between 347 and 504 unarmed people were killed by U.S. Army soldiers from Company C, 1st Battalion, 20th Infantry Regiment...(Wikipedia)

As we march, I see some standing water. There might be leeches that would attach themselves to you, and then you must screw them out of your skin. They become circles of blood. You never know how deep it might be or what might be in the water. You close your eyes and prepare to be bitten by something. I walk with my weapon above my head.

Jimmy Boudwin is lagging today; he looks hazy and a little high, eyes sliding out of his head. He's a stoner too.

Wee Willie has pep in his step, and he almost seems to lead us through the jungle. His limbs are going every which way and he appears to be whistling again.

"Told you about that damned whistling, didn't I? And turn off that damn flashlight." barks the Lieutenant. Just then, fire, Bobby, with the flashlight was hit in the head, dead. Wee Willie stops whistling.

Wee Willie could give away position, but I don't think he's thinking about that now. Even though he's in this hellhole, in his mind he's strolling down the street in New York City without a care. There is something irrepressible and strong about Wee Willie at times. Everyone else can be overly concerned about something and he will come in ignoring the enemy, whistling.

He seems to be forever on the periphery of things, looking in, able to move and dodge and leave danger at its door. It also means that he is oblivious to some shit too. I like to be close to him in the formation, like I am today, because it seems like nothing will happen to him. Wee Willie was the same on the basketball court; when the rest of his teammates were scared, he would just whisper "let's get down, man; we can play with this team."

In the projects, basketball was a life-or-death cause. I have seen underdog players from other teams stabbed after games or some would twist broken 40 beer ounce bottles in the opposing team's faces. Some were shot and killed. If they did not win the game, they were intent to win the fight. There was reason to fear if your team beat the neighborhood icons. Wee Willie never feared anyone on the court because he was fast as greased lightening and he played with a "heart as big as all outdoors."

He never feared the other team or the challenge of being against the wall. He always thought he could come out from the wall and win. And he's carried that attitude to Vietnam, always willing to engage, never thinking he will catch the bullet.

Father, father… we don't need to escalate.

We are always searching for the illusive town where robust enemies stand with machine guns. Most of the Viet Cong I get to see are helpless. We must see them all as potential killers.

"Cover!"

Taking fire. Wee Willie scampers behind a tree, holding his weapon, attacking back. I dive for cover and Bubba Cee stands in the middle of the road screaming and shouting. Lieutenant

Wrong reaches up and grabs Bubba Cee by the back and pulls him to safety. Most of us are in position, crouching, returning fire. I am on my belly, firing, afraid to look.

Jimmy has just been patched up and sent back to the front. Jimmy's gun is jammed; before I can get to him, he takes one in his arm and falls to the jungle floor.

"Man down!"

The frantic screams in the radio for Medevac begin. I can hear the helicopters and see the platforms being set. You hear helicopters in your brain all night long but when you need them to come and take your buddy away, they seem fade into the blue smoke of distance, then appear again quickly again. They are our saviors.

"Man down!"

Jimmy is squirming and crying; I can barely hear him through the gunshots. Somebody has to help my friend Jimmy. I can't stop shooting because everyone else is firing and I have to defend.

"Somebody has to fucking help Jimmy!" I am screaming at the top of my lungs.

"Stretcher!"

Nobody is coming for long seconds, but I can't peel back because I might lose my life in the process. I keep firing and firing. Medevac arrives before I know it, and I help pull Jimmy, who is still breathing and talking shit, onto the stretcher and into the bay of the helicopter. The blades of the copter continue to cut the night into slithers. Smoke is every fucking where and I can't hear a damned thing. Jimmy is shaking but he gives me a half-assed smile as I load him. His eyes are just about to close, and his skin is as pale as hell. His ugly, red pimples are inflamed, and his breathing is beyond labored. I try to put my face in front of his so he can see me and stay alive.

I watch the helicopter from my defensive crouch for a second and then return to fire. It really was less than ten minutes, but it felt so much longer. Jimmy is put on a different stretcher and taken to the helicopter. They have surprised us, destroyed major South Vietnamese strongholds, attacked General Eastmorland's base, and made progress, catching us, before the Marines begin to resist at the American embassy.

At night, I hear nothing but gunshots and laughter from Bubba Cee and his friends. They hide their grins with their hands. These automatic weapons, and bombs are unlike the pop-pop of the handguns I would hear at home. I hear the bullets whistling all night long. I must stay up, guarding the others, with my weapon at the ready. The perimeter has been drawn and the traps, to protect us, have been planted.

CHAPTER NINE

Days later, people count the dead, stumble over bodies, and think about being alive and contacting home. The deep smell of death gets in your body and does not allow you to vomit it up—it travels with you, deep like a bass solo that will never stop; eventually it gives you a piercing pain in your chest, stabbing with carefully honed knives of death.

"Hey, Richard. How's that letter coming?" Majour shouts through flying dirt as we get our backpacks on and prepare for the day's trek.

Majour turns his bird-like head. I can barely make out his green uniform in all the dust. I give him a nod. My legs pain but there's no bottle of pain reliever and my arms ache like exposed nerves. This is not the time for human kindness. Time to lift them up and put 'em down. Yesterday, I found a picture of a dead brother's wife and a letter to his wife in case he died. I pick it up and think of some way of mailing it to her.

Majour is pressing me to write a letter to a lady friend back home.

"I got most of it done," I say, standing.

"Oh, you do?"

"Yeah, it starts out with a little review of your past with her and then it goes into something like this... our relationship has been through different levels and the friendship has been sustaining, but if it's not asking too much, I want you to consider being more than a friend to me. How could I ask that being in

Vietnam? It's precisely because I am here that I need to know. And then it goes on…"

"Damn. You're a Shakespearean fool. When you get back to the States, you need to put some things down on paper."

Mortar shells rain in the near distance.

"Let's move it out, men."

I really feel like the blind following the sightless.

Some of us seem to be waiting… waiting… for a few ounces of lead caught forever between barrel and head…

It might be writing the letters and dealing with emotions, but today, more than ever, I don't want to die. I want to live. I have to move past the static state in my mind. I can almost smell the trees amid the smoke.

Bubba Cee and the boys are always seeking new recruits for their little band of un-merry men. They would love for me to join them.

Majour loves the debate and not the conclusion. He really should be a college professor. Back home, he asked me questions that I would have to think about for days. I think he did it on purpose, to make me develop my mind.

"Do you think it's right that little children are killing our men?" Richard asks.

"Who would think that's right? Killing itself, even in a time of war, is the enemy, not the people," Majour says.

"You should have become a fucking minister. Convenient to think that way."

"Why is it convenient? Convenient for who, motherfucker?"

"You. There's no commitment then. You don't have to take a side," Bubba Cee says.

"What uniform am I wearing, bitch?"

"The good old U.S. of A."

"I already chose a side then, hoe."

"Why I gotta be all that?"

"Cause you're acting like a bitch. You know you can't win me over with that dime-store psychology shit."

"You're a tough one, Major, but you know that we have to fight fire with fire."

"The spirit of the people is greater than the man's technology. That's Huey P. Newton—leader of the Black Panther Party said at Temple University in 1979 in the gymnasium. I was there."

"You talk a lot of shit."

Jimmy is stumbling a few feet away; they patched him up and sent him back—to the land of the stinking red clay, here in the Khe Shan region.

It turns out the wounds weren't as serious as the brass thought. Bubba Cee signals to the Professor and they meet up behind what was once a tree. They whisper to one another as they continue to glare at Majour. Some other new recruits join them, and they all seem to share one look of recrimination.

I turn away from the burn of words and try to sleep. I have not dreamt since I've been in Vietnam. When I was at home, before I left, I would have nightmares—nothing as bad as the horrible images of war; war images dance like hobgoblins now, taking up the background and the foreground of my dreams. When I wake, battle images are still there. I see floaters in the same shape as the hobgoblins; there are guns and the empty forms of small Vietnamese children filled in with blood. These figures dance around, intimidating and robbing me of sleep. The figures sometimes run and when they do, their heads fly off, leaving electrical wire sprouting out of their necks. The wires send sparks into the blackest sky I have ever seen.

Wee Willie comes over, kicking up dirt, waking me.

"What's good, man?" I ask him.

"Nothing's good. I'm over here with you."

"Well, the two of us might as well be good then. What we do with one another is the most important thing, Richard says.

"You got it, brother," Willie says as a comeback, "the Whites are getting a little restless."

"I know. They seem a little jittery. Like we give a fuck what they do. If we wanted to tell somebody, they wouldn't believe us any damned way," Richard says.

"I know, brother. Nobody believes the Black man, not in the military anyway, Willie shoots back.

"There are certain things that are always true about the U.S. of A."

"Yeah, Ellison was right in that book. *Invisible man* —we will always be invisible to them. And sometimes, I like the fact that they don't see us," Willie says.

"You got it. But they're always visible to us. Too visible with their red faces and outdated ideas."

"And they think everything they say is profound…"

I see dreamlike shadows, rifles pointed to heads in the blueness, small children run for the protection of partial walls that are blown to bits. Women shriek and put their hands to their eyes, unable to see the unspeakable horror. I shudder, my body shaking with images. My spine trembles. I can see silhouettes of their bodies as bombs continue to light up the sky for their last seconds.

Bubba Cee and the others are jumping, slapping high five. The flashes of bullets illuminate the fists rising in triumph and I can't tell the enemy from the enemy.

News from home cuts deep in letters from Ma. She has not missed a day of sending me the front page of the *New Times* York. Her descriptions make me miss the city. She keeps me appraised on all demonstrations, civil and anti-war movements. She also tells me about this group I would like to join, the BLACK PANTHERS. My mother mails me their ten-point program. This is something, instead of the Gettysburg Address, all school children should memorize.

Her words have a tempo. Somehow, Bubba Cee gets a copy of the *New York Times*' front page—I think it came folded up in the middle of his last letter from home. There is a picture of a girl, running, with most of her skin burned off by napalm, trying to go down a road to seek shelter. The look on her face is horrible—she is unaware that her skin is dripping and that there are patches of blood and raw flesh falling from her. Yellow and purple smoke from bombs surround the girl. She is quintessentially naked and her flesh is falling from her. The cry from her mouth is heard even though there is no sound. She is surrounded by exploding bombs, buildings shattering, and burning airplanes.

I hear talk about the demonstrations. Ma writes to me about the college campuses and what's happening at Columbia University with the Students for a Democratic Society, the Black Panthers, and the Weathermen. She sends lead stories from the New York Times' or just headlines that she carefully cuts out with the jump to the story included behind her personal letter.

Like electric shock, marches stimulate. There seem to be protests everywhere—tragedy at Kent State and the picture of the girl screaming in front of police fire over the body of a what could have been a friend, a fellow demonstrator. This coupled with the war on drugs at home, makes things very complicated. She gives me every detail from the CBS news imbedded in her prose. They are locking up niggers in South Jamaica like bothersome flies. Ma believes in Walter Cronkite, like I do. Even the trees seem to resent us here.

Nobody else seems to be affected by the picture of the girl like I am, because she reminds me of the little girls in the projects, I would see in the vest pocket playgrounds, so vulnerable and alone. I can't get her expression, aimless movement and dripping limbs out of my thoughts. Most of us are numb, to see the world plunge itself into this canyon of this war is too much. It seems like the little girl is screaming in my ear as her skin chars.

It is the size of the dog in the fight/and the size of the fight in the dog.

CHAPTER TEN

I watch the helicopter from my defensive crouch for a second and then return to fire. They have surprised us, destroyed major South Vietnamese strongholds, attacked General Westmorland's base, and made progress, catching us by surprise, before we start to resist at the American embassy.

The war is getting complex, and people seem to be losing what little minds they come over her with. There are constant delusions, men that think they are lot when they are really a little. If you go into battle with that idea, it may be a death knell.

I see something dark moving in the distance.

I know Wee Willie's form; I've seen his side view one thousand times, ditty-bopping out of the building in the morning. We lived near each other; my building was about one hundred feet in front of his. Before my mother's move to Union Hall Street, I would wait to see him coming out of the house to play basketball. Wee Willie did not walk, he streaked down the street. I would always try to match is walking speed but to no avail. I would come out, trying to match his speed. His motor was always on high.

I turn over and over in mud. There, just beyond the edge of fire, is Wee Willie. There is no one with him. That's a good sign. He walks over, shaking his head like a rag doll.

"I just had to see it, man. I just had to see it for myself. You could tell me about it, or I could read the shit, in the *New York*

Times, but I just had to see the damned thing for myself. These motherfuckers have lost all sense of what they used to be—they are not fucking human beings anymore, man! They will kill anything moving or crawling. I saw them raid a village. They just shot every motherfucker without searching them for weapons or knives or anything—just took the families out, one by one and killed them. Cut their fucking ears off and hacked at the limbs or dicks for souvenirs. This shit is sick, man! We need to get out of here as soon as we can. These are some sick fucks."

"I know, but we got to maintain and realize where we are. In the joint, you eventually realize that you're behind bars. It takes a while for your mind to adjust to it, but your ass is in a cell and there are bars the fuck in front of you. These motherfuckers with the shit on their shoulders control our existence. That's easy. Just like prison or marriage, man, you got to have a warden all the time."

No one will admit that the Viet Cong are getting stronger. I guess trumped-up kill ratios are supposed to make us feel better, but we know they are strengthening with each victory. Lieutenant Wrong delivers a speech.

"I don't know what most of you are thinking, as we walk through the jungle with motherfucking gooks all around but there is a purpose here. We are sharing our way of life, our system of government, our freedoms with the Indochinese people and because they do not recognize the beauty of our system, we must force it down their throats. They will be better off with democracy, like taking cod liver oil, it's bitter but good for you. War does not taste good…"

Bubba Cee looks away, kicking the mud, not listening.

As it gets deeper and deeper into the war, my mind almost stops working. I am numb from the senseless marching through red clay. I hear things from people about discharges and ways to get back home but the world has split—the world of muddy experience and my memory of horror. In Vietnam horror and experience become one. It's like reckless driving—the world seems unreal until you hit something or someone, then you wake up. I feel heaviness in the center of my chest each day. There are pieces of skulls and husks of bodies on the ground everywhere and I feel like a tree is boring into my chest late at night.

The letter for Majour was a tough one but he came back with an even bigger task. He wanted me to write to his father and explain what he's doing in Vietnam. His dad is suffering from Alzheimer's sundowning effect, and he gets really confused.

Dear Dad,

I know that things are confusing, but I wanted to try to break all this war stuff down. Basically, the United States of America thinks it can tell other people how to run their government and what to think. These little people have a strong will, and they have different kinds of fighting techniques, some we have never seen before. Besides, this is their nation—would you let someone come in and tell you how to run your household? Well, that's what we're trying to do but we're having some difficulty. It's not only the terrain but these people have a heart, a collective will that we didn't plan on. They also have not been stopped by Agent Orange or napalm. I think they have an idea of what this napalm/Agent Orange stuff can do. It's supposed to destroy generations—not just the people we see but their children and generations after. In many ways, we have bolstered the enemy's spirits by telling lies about their lack of aggression and inability to fight a war. They have something to prove.

America doesn't want to admit that they underestimated the resolve of the Viet Cong, and as the world's leading Democracy, part of our job is to be the world's policemen.

Soldiers are pawns.

I try to save my own ass, keep my head down and not talk too much. The other thing is, I stay to myself like I always have. The White man don't like their Blackfolks to be too articulate, so I talk to Richard and a few others and keep my nose clean.

Just like back home, an intelligent Black man is hated by his own kind and the others. Try to concentrate on memories, the past, something that will anchor you and make you remember. Look at pictures of the family and your kids and then everything will come back to you.

Your son,
Majour

Dear Majour
You are a good son. Be careful.
Your daddy

Jimmy Boudwin, barely alive from injury and shooting dope, is stinking. He smells like a cross between a skunk and a decomposing raccoon. I breathe shallow breaths, so the feeling of imminent death won't overtake my lungs and make the drill in my chest deepen. Jimmy Boudwin got used to smelling sour like that when he was shooting dope back in South Jamaica.

"What is it? Jimmy!"

"Yeah, yeah... I need to talk to you. I need a big favor. I know you said that you don't write to children but, you know," he says, scratching the crook of his arm.

"What is it?"

"I need you to write to a son I've never seen before."

"Now you know I don't want to touch that one with a fork."

"Come on, you and I go back like two Cadillacs."

"Yeah, but lying to a child?"

"It won't be lies. It'll be the God's honest."

"What do you want to say?"

"I want to apologize for not coming to see him and to tell him that I might never see him because I might get shot over here, you know, sort of a dear John to a child." Jimmy's eyes are pleading and empty at the same time.

"I might make an exception in your case, but I won't lie."

"I know, but suppose you never saw your dad and then he dies without a word."

"Tough task, buddy. Go away and come back in about two hours and I'll have something for you."

He puts his head down and slouches away. Maybe we're just too close to one another here. My mother keeps sending the New York Times' front pages.

Martin goes out on the balcony for a smoke… shots ring out. His body slumps over, his head explodes as he falls forward onto concrete and out of the protection of Andy Young and Reverend Ralph Abernathy. My mother's New York Times pages inform us.

The assassination of Dr. Martin Luther King Jr.; slain in April in Memphis—two months after the My Lai massacre; one month after LBJ announces that he will not run…

The New York Times pages come a little bit late, but I can follow what is happening in America.

Friday, April 5th, 1968: Martin Luther King shot dead

The American black civil rights leader, Dr. Martin Luther King, has been assassinated.

Dr. King was shot dead in the southern U.S. city of Memphis, Tennessee, where he was to lead a march of sanitation workers protesting low wages and poor working conditions, says Walter Cronkite on C.B.S. nightly news.

He was shot in the neck as he stood on a hotel balcony and died in hospital soon afterwards.

Reverend Jesse Jackson was on the balcony with Dr. King when the single shot rang out.

"He had just bent over. I reckon if he had been standing up he would not have been hit in the face," said Mr. Jackson.

"I ask every citizen to reject the blind violence that has taken Dr. King…" President Lyndon Johnson says in a speech from the White House, directly after the shooting of Martin Luther King, Jr., in an effort to stop the rioting in Detroit, Chicago, New York and all the major cities with significant Black populations.I am a stone. The headlines from Tennessee come over Radio Hanoi and in the *New York Times'* front pages my mother sends daily. The Professor manages to get a picture of Martin after the first bullet hit and he passes it around the unit. He is the only one with any understanding of the situation on the streets of America, but I can't be sure about his heart. Professor seems a little weary, beaten down by the lack of thinking of the others some days and his legs tell the story. Whenever he is limping, he is coming back from their tents, where they have tried to beat the logic out of him.

I can envision Martin falling from the balcony. I see him in my mind's eye, a huge, dark doll falling from a hotel terrace again and again. Shapiro looks at the ground a lot and tries to explain it away. He looks almost as shaken as I am. His flat, slate-gray eyes are full of apology.

"Sorry about what happened to King," he says, holding his puny member.

"Yeah. Don't be sorry, be careful."

"I know you're angry and all."

"You have no idea. I can't put what I feel into words you would understand."

"I know. But he was bound to get it sooner or later. He was asking for it"

I feel my feet and hands start to move. I hold.

"I'm sorry, really I am."

"Yeah."

I turn and move further into the wilderness.

My mother's last letters have pictures of Coretta Scott King and the children. Coretta is implacable behind her black veil.

And I bend over and retch while in a windy city motel in Memphis… how many others have thought about this? They send threatening letters and gifts of hate, make assassination threats over the phone. Martin carried these threats and the love of Coretta and his children with him, knowing each day might be his last in Selma streets, or Birmingham backyards.

"MARTIN LUTHER KING JR. HAS BEEN ASSASINATED IN TENNESSEE"

For me—this is only the morning after Martin has been shot—nothing else matters. My mother sends me pictures of the burning cities and deep down inside, this sparks a hidden fear that my country may erupt. Somehow, the Whites in the unit get a picture of King in a casket and they draw big lips and Stephin Fetchit eyes, big and exaggerated on King's picture and circulate the photo. This is just the type of stereotyping and terror that Martin Luther King Jr. fought against. Shapiro comes over and puts his hand on my shoulder for a long minute. The confederate flags fly high at camp.

"We knew the forces of fascism would triumph one day. He knew it and everyone around him knew it too."

"Doesn't make it feel any better."

"I know. When you lose a voice like that, a leader like that, nothing can take his place."

"But another leader."

"Do you see one? I don't."

"Jessie Jackson—no, none of the profundity. I don't really see anybody with the kind of depth Martin had."

"Just wait though. It might happen."

"Thanks, Shapiro. Thanks."

He takes his hand off my shoulder, but I can still feel all of his fingers.

The universe is slammed shut and I can only see Martin with French cuffed shirts and cuff links, silk pants and a bullet hole in his brain. For the first time in months, last night, I dreamt thousands of hotel balconies, ornate, iron, like they have in Tennessee. There are roses intertwined with the wrought iron, White people across the street pointing to the shooter. When I first saw Martin, he had on a silk suit and combat boots with his arm around Coretta's shoulders. He walked so straight.

CHAPTER ELEVEN

MY LETTER HOME TO MYSELF

The events of home are taking its toll on me. There is nothing I can do about the assassination of King. The streets erupt and my people loot and pour out into the street. A river of blood runs through the concrete at home, and we will smash windows and steal what the White people took from us a long time ago. Ever since I was a boy, I would watch the news and carry the stories and people in the stories on my shoulders, as if I could do something to change the world, and soon I would find myself alone, in my room, on the emotional island, surrounded by the absurdity of Martin's death that makes me realize that America is spinning, spiraling toward an end that I cannot save them from. No one can save us but ourselves.

The men from the unit still come to me for letters and I try to oblige them. This helps me keep my mind together—the look of one more decimated body and I might fucking lose it. Scribbling words down is a comforting feeling.

I can be a lot of things but the one thing I can't be is THERE. I am here, dodging bullets... and trying to make the world safe for democracy... oh that was World War II...

I start the letter to Tina for Bubba Cee but for some reason I can't finish the damned thing...

Weeks pass. Whites and Blacks get tired of being at each other's throats and Wee Willie is weakening but he skillfully makes the Whites think that their ideas are not so crazy. The assassination of Martin has sobered people even here. I still see flags of the old south in front of tents and the looks to match but some of the rancor is gone, the steely edge of hatred has dulled a little bit. After all, we must fight together when we go to the front.

"Anti-War Demonstrations continue all across the U.S."
Actual article from *The New York Times*.

News comes from home about the anti-war movement; my mother writes, flooding me with more and more information, information about each college campus. She used to be a teacher. I love her when she lets the intelligent side of her show but since my father went away, she is sullen. Stale memory rules her now and she is seldom as bright as she once was but every now and again, illumination pokes through the fog.

Her letters cry because she has given in to strong drink, so the lucid passages are few; most of her writing has incomprehensible letters and illegible paragraphs with drunken symbols at the end. She reads the *New York Times* every day, like my father did when he lived with us. The letters make my stomach jump when I think of those shaky scripts, but morning comes, and the daily war/march continues. It seems like an endless funeral dirge, and I am trapped between two soldiers unable to do anything to help the situations back home.

To protect myself, I return to the familiar in my mind. This is the way I try to go to sleep every night—rocking in the chair of my familiar. It doesn't always work but each night I work on it, trying to reconstruct pleasant memories of home. There are moments with the boys, but I always miss more than my mind can collect. My mind goes back to beginnings. I travel to childhood. In the center of my daydream, Sandra is emerging from the brick. She is dancing between two buildings wearing tights with red sequins. Sandra has breasts that protrude—she tries to hold them in with the restriction of her black top, but the breasts are too full. They dance and jiggle their light skin just above the restriction of the blouse. She is holding a bundle and I can't see the face, but it looks like a child and the child is sweating a little and smiling. The child emits a high-pitched squeal. Around her, I can feel the heat from flames of enemy fire. I see her every night in my mind before the whistling sounds of landing bombs break my daydreams apart.

Sometimes I see floaters, little bright lights near the muzzle of my M-16. When I'm looking at something dark, like a leaf, it may flicker and become a light-blue flash that throbs. For a moment, I can't see anything. I know they aren't real, but they garner my attention—I can't wave the dots away.

The ghosts are visible in Vietnam. They are all around, walking; they could be old women or children with bayonets. On days like this, I hunger for the bullet…

"Mayday. Mayday."

There is a barrage of fucking fire. We walked into another one. Bubba Cee is down, near me, and I walk over to him, straddle his body, and fire every fucking round I have.

"Ahhh… take that, you fucking gooks…." Rat-tat-tat…

The firing continues. Men drop. Smoke surrounds. I can't see anything—flashback to Harlem in an alleyway: I'm pinned against the wall; a fourteen-year-old has a gun in my mouth—am I in a Harlem hallway or...

I keep shooting. The steel of the M-16 has become my hands. Bubba Cee is moaning beneath me. I can see blood spurting from his knee. He's making sounds so I know he's alive. Jimmy Boudwin is down too, grabbing his arm.

I can hear the helicopter in the distance, but it seems far away and close at the same time. When I look up, the helicopter door opens, and a medic runs out. The fourteen-year-old in my mind disappears for a moment. My head feels like it has been through a wash cycle.

I check Bubba Cee and as I fire, the fourteen-year-old kid begins to drag Bubba Cee across the ground to the helicopter. I help with one arm and continue to fire with the other. Jimmy Boudwin is still down. The medical personnel can barely move—they are pinned by fire coming from all sides; their eyes are broken saucers. I crawl between the medic's legs and drag Jimmy Boudwin to the bay for the helicopter. The fourteen-year-old, in my mind, disappears.

The blades of the copter seem to fade away. I look up for a second and then feel something glancing against my leg. I don't have time to inspect; although my legs are weary, I must keep standing and fighting. I need cover. I find a ragged brick wall and run behind it. I duck down and hear the bullets pounding the concrete; someone must be getting through. I get up again and start to fire into the black smoke of the Vietnam afternoon.

By night-time, the battle stops a little. I look at my leg; there is a lot of blood, but I don't see any bone. Bubba Cee comes back with a bandaged knee. I'm lucky this time; there's nothing to do but wrap a tourniquet around it and stop the bleeding. The bullet grazed my motherfucking ass. Jimmy is up again, firing. My mother sends me the story on the death of Robert Fitzgerald Kennedy on June 6th, 1968:

"In the back tunnels... of the main ballroom... Robert Kennedy has been shot... at the Democratic National Convention... Robert Kennedy... the brother of John Fitzgerald Kennedy has been shot..."
"Kennedy succumbed to extensive brain damage caused when his assassin fired eight shots at point-blank range.
Death came at 1.44 a.m. and was attributed to a bullet that entered his head behind the right ear. Kennedy was not able to build back up tissue after the trauma of last night and the surgery this morning," said Frank Mankiewicz, Kennedy's press secretary who made the official announcement.

President Johnson was informed immediately of the death and proclaimed a day of national mourning.

Then, at one minute before two a.m. (PDT) Frank Mankiewicz said: "I have a short announcement to make; then he looked down and referred to his text:

"I have a short announcement to read, which I will read at this time. Senator Robert Francis Kennedy died at 1.44 a.m., today, June 6, 1968. With Senator Kennedy at the time of his death was his wife, Ethel, his sister, Patricia Lawford, his brother-in-law, Stephen Smith, and his sister-in-law, Mrs. John F. Kennedy. He was 42 years old."

How long shall they kill our prophets?

I look over the hill near our base and there is nothing but a black sky. It's almost as if all the blueness has been sucked out and will never return. The sky should not be the color of smoke.

Bubba Cee grins a demonic grin as he walks over.

"I told you America wasn't ready for all of this."

"If you can shoot a candidate dead at the Democratic National Convention, then what do we have here? America is coming apart and this war is the knife driving a wedge through people. If there are assorted nuts there, then what can I hope to return to?"

"Yeah, you may sound good to your own mind."

"All this integration stuff. Too soon."

"You're a fucking idiot."

"I know, but I'm right. The country has to destroy all of your icons first and then they can belch and start all over."

"Like a Moloch."

"Yeah, you could call it that. What the fuck is a Moloch?"

"A monster."

"Yeah, you see Martin Luther King and his boys were pushing America too hard. Just like with the stock market—there is always a correction."

"Fuck you, Bubba Cee."

"Yeah, but you're going to have to fuck me without Robert Kennedy."

I lunge at his bad knee and before I know it, we're grappling in the dirt. I'm climbing on top of him but he's fighting to win. I reach up for his face and scratch him from ear to mouth, then I back up and throw right cross after right cross. Bubba Cee tries to duck but he's too slow and my blows register. He's almost out as I hit him again, but he backs up and charges like a hungry bull. He lunges and head butts. I'm numb but I reach out and grab the blob in front of me. I wrestle him to the ground, to the mud…

PARIS PEACE TALKS… CONTINUE… The United States and Vietnam officials are initiating talks to end the war… negotiations are going quite slowly as there are many areas of disagreement…

Bubba Cee and Jimmy Boudwin come back to the company in a few days, after being stitched up.

I doctor on myself; my wounds are easy. President Johnson has ordered a new offensive and more boys and girls will be called up.

I must write Bubba Cee's mother and tell her about the wounds he incurred in battle and thank her for the articles from the paper. I pick up Bubba Cee's picture of a thin, pretty, freckled faced girl. Jimmy Boudwin needs me to write a letter too.
    The next time on base, the newly rejuvenated Bubba Cee starts some shit. They bandage him up and put him back in the field. Jimmy Boudwin takes a little bit longer to return but he's back now with only part of his brain, which is a dangerous thing. He looks a little strange, but I know he enjoyed the drugs in the makeshift hospital. He leans and never stands straight, almost as if he is about to go into a nod at any moment, as if he is feeling an invisible wind.

"Yeah, these niggers ain't never had three squares and clean clothes every month. This is living *good* for them. They love the military," Bubba Cee says.

"But that's their right," says the Professor.

"They're taking our rights and our rank; medals that belong to White soldiers are going to them."

"Well, if they earn it on the field of battle, they should get it."

"Bullshit. They give them preferential treatment even in the military. They get all the college scholarships and the access to the military and then when the little jungle bunnies are in the service, they give them all the awards. McNamara got a plan for them, to let them in the Marines at a lower rate."

"I don't know. You see everything through your own perspective. That McNamara plan will get a lot of folks killed—one hundred thousand folks. Equal opportunity at being shot. You like the conclusions of your own mind?"

"And what's wrong with that? Didn't Einstein like his own thoughts?"

"I guess but he worked harder than you and didn't let his prejudices stop him from thinking clearly."

"You think that's what I do?"

"You got that old American illness, the need to put down what you can't understand."

"That's what you think of me? A backwoods redneck?"

I hear the scuffling in the distance. They shuffle in the dirt and a few enlisted men come out to watch. Shapiro walks by, shaking his head. Bubba rights himself and throws a straight jab that the Professor dodges and counters with a right cross. Bubba Cee turns red as hell and grits his teeth, unable to accept defeat. I squint, as Bubba Cee charges the Professor. He uses his head for a battering ram, hitting the Professor in his stomach. The Professor bangs Bubba Cee in the back of his neck, pushes him to the ground and begins to stomp the shit out of him.

Someone starts a real fire, and a circle encloses the two men; they can barely stand up now, but their fists are at their jaws, awaiting release. They slip and slide through the darkness. The others watch. Their blows are sloppy—they miss. I can barely see through the baggy green legs of the enlisted men. Some are off doing other jobs.

I enter into the sleeping bag of memory, closing my eyes to everything around. At night, I feel like I'm on a cliff and if I close my eyes too tightly, I'll fall off.

I'm thinking about my boys: Headley, Charlie Leslie, Wee Willie—what in the hell happened to them? I know Headley's in his heaven; Charlie is in the hospital but that Wee Willie, he's an elusive one.

The next morning we're off, marching. There is water ahead and I instantly hold my weapon high and follow the first man into the pond. There is no telling how deep the water will be until you see the line on the chest of the first dude. Right now, the water is almost chest high. The first guy is about five-seven. It would be different on me. The water here is filled with all kinds of crawling shit that might attach to your leg. The smell is too putrid to categorize. I keep my head up and walk making sure my rifle does not touch.

A few steps past the water. Gunfire! We're pinned down. I shoot into the smoke, creating more fire. We must hold our position. I dive behind a huge rock that used to be a building. Like Floyd Patterson, I do a peek-a-boo sticking my neck out and firing and then hiding behind the rock again. There is massive return and we hit the ground, trying not to catch our death.

I see Bubba Cee standing there, shooting, like he's crazy.

Someone needs to tackle him and take him out of harm's way. He is losing his fucking mind, yelling, and giving up the position at the same time.

"I'll get you, gook motherfuckers!" he yells.

Professor jumps out and takes Bubba Cee down like a defensive back. The fire continues. We are fucking pinned. Lieutenant Wrong is screaming into the walkie-talkie for "back up... back up!"

The helicopter sound splits the air minutes later. I've eaten enough clay. Bullets fly left and right, whizzing about my ears, almost grazing my head.

Ammo low. M-16 jams. I kneel, grab some ammunition, and reload. The weapon jerks me back in the side again and again until it builds up a rhythm of fire and smoke, injuring the firing wound callous on my chest. Some are being taken in sheets to the landing area and the helicopter. Majour stands over me.

"It's over, hommie. For now. You all right? You've been hit but you'll make it."

"Yeah, if I can just stop shaking."

"I know. My arms are still like leaves. This war shit is for the birds."

"I don't know how long I was even on the ground."

"Good thing. Johnson and Murphy got it. They're gone. Shapiro's all right. He made it. You been shot in the shoulder, but it doesn't look too bad."

"Damn. I couldn't see for looking."

"Too much smoke. Too much fire."

My stomach feels like it's going to tear apart; there are too many memories. I remember all the men when they first arrived and I flash images, pictures of their fresh faces changing into Hogarth masks.

I embrace everything around me, all the hunched-over skeletons and decomposing skulls, they are a part of my new self, the disemboweled-self, given birth to in the jungle. The darkness is a part of me, and I must hug it like mud sealed to my skin. The fire and men hiding in holes surround. There is nothing to lick but flames.

Later that night, after they bandage me up, I see Wee Willie. His face is obtuse looking, and he is laughing, with something in his hands. Wee Willie stops before me and waves an object in the air before he disappears in the jungle. Probably the ears of the Viet Cong but—they are the wrong color?

Wee Willie is waving something red and pink! The American men struggle behind him; their faces are contorted masks of Gothic death. They throw their hands at Wee Willie's back, protesting something but they have no voices. Through the film of sleep, I notice Shapiro and the Professor chasing Wee Willie but where is Bubba Cee and the others? Wee Willie is running like he did on the basketball court—they will never catch that nigger. He is Fast, the Destroyer.

The Army awarded Bubba Cee the Congressional Medal of Honor for his actions on the field of battle. The Professor and the others were reported MIA. Two months later, the military said Wee Willie was killed by a "Bouncing Betty" (grenade). A chaplain wrote the letter to Wee Willie's mother, Audrey Waters:

Dear Ms. Waters,
  By now, you have been officially notified of the death of your son. First off, let me apologize for writing you on such a

sad occasion, but I wanted to share a few tidbits about "Wee Willie."

He was a deep thinker and he loved you, Anthony, and every member of his family. His fondest wish was to return home, finish high school and finally attend college. Above all, he wanted to make you proud of him.

Wee Willie was ethical, strong, and dedicated to the dream of America. He knew there was some hypocrisy and downright lies but he was willing to dedicate himself to the war effort despite all that.

I heard he came from modest circumstances, but you would have never known that. Most of all, I will remember his dedication to the unit, his unabashed love of his fellow man and his love of this life. Life is ever changing for all of us—we know that and still our faith, values and family must remain paramount.

This was true for William—he carried a picture with him of his blood family, but he considered everyone a member of his extended family and he held the unit, the brigade, his mother, and all of the faces of this confused country in his heart.

This war has separated us all, but I will always remember Wee Willie's undeniable smile, effervescent spirit and belief in his fellow man.

Humbly yours,
Chaplain Jeter

Cold rains make you think about friends. I try to dodge the raindrops, but they just seem to get larger, but not large enough for me to climb in.

I return to the envelope of sleep and feel some pressure near my forehead, then liquid seems to flow all over my neck and chest; hands hold me down. I try to get up again and again, but they press on me and push me back to the cot. Some of their fingernails dig into my chest; before I can begin to breathe, they move their grimy hands up and cover my mouth. I am without air, but I can feel something sharp against my neck and I fight and squirm just before my head feels like it's about to fly off. Butterflies seem to come from my neck, fluttering out into the deep blue sky, then the dull cutting pain of an almost electric shock.

THE END